Page Turner

Rayanne Sinclair

Hopetoun Publishing
Edmonds, Washington

Rayanne Sinclair

PAGE TURNER
Rayanne Sinclair
Copyright © 2015 by Rayanne Sinclair

HOPETOUN PUBLISHING
Edmonds, Washington

For more information about this and other books by Rayanne Sinclair, visit www.rayannesinclair.com

Print ISBN 978-0-9897502-4-0
Electronic ISBN 978-0-9897502-5-7

This is dedicated to the ones I know

Acknowledgements

Once again, my thanks go to Nancy Wick, Beth Jusino, Jenn Reese, Laura Vowles, and Kathy Burge for contributing their talents to this, my third novel. These professionals have walked with me through the ups and downs of a writer's life over the last two years. With this book, I also welcomed a talented new team member, Stephanie Cooper. I only wish all of these women could see the larger picture I get to see—that of how well their skills and insights blend together to confirm a final product.

Lastly, I want to say that *Page Turner* holds a special place for me among my novels because its primary setting is where I spent my undergraduate years. Throughout the writing of this novel, I had the privilege of seeing the Ohio State Buckeyes football team through a trying but successful 2014 season to take the Big Ten Championship game, the Sugar Bowl, and the Bowl Championship Series (BCS). I acknowledge their 2015 national championship victory with a simple, "Oh come let's sing Ohio's praise and songs to Alma Mater raise."

CHAPTER 1

The devil is in the details, to be sure. But Page Holden was beginning to wonder if the devil was also orchestrating much broader schemes as she stared at the envelope with a return address from Ohio State University's admissions office.

Having spent the last year providing private piano lessons in her small apartment several blocks off High Street in Columbus, Page didn't know if she could handle another rejection from the graduate School of Music. After graduating in the class of 1960 from Ohio Wesleyan, she sat out the past year after getting the bad news from Ohio State, scratching out a living while waiting to see if the second time around would be a charm.

Now twenty-three years old, Page was more than eager to get on with her studies. Her dream of getting a master's degree in music and becoming a concert pianist seemed to be nothing more than that after the last year, which had gone on for what seemed like an eternity.

Pulling out a paring knife from the kitchen drawer, she took in a deep breath and slit the envelope. As she drew out the letter and unfolded it, her eyes first landed on the date of May 1, 1961, and then caught the word "congratulations" in the first line. With one hand over her heart, she exhaled and read the entire document. The tears were rolling down her cheeks as she lifted her eyes toward the ceiling and whispered, "Praise God from whom all blessings flow!"

As all former feelings of discouragement seemed to fly out the open window of her first-floor studio apartment, they were immediately replaced with overwhelming joy. She found herself waltzing out of the small kitchenette and into the one larger room she occupied most of the time. From there she floated into the small bathroom and caught a glimpse of herself in the mirror above the vanity. For a moment, Page couldn't remember when she looked so pretty, despite being perpetually unhappy with her short brown hair and bangs that always seemed to fall across her left eye. However, today she saw past all that to focus on the glint in her light brown eyes and the rose color upon her cheeks that seemed to match her lips. Smiling back at herself, she also had to concede that although she didn't have perfect teeth, at least she had thick, sweeping brown eyelashes.

Looking down at the acceptance letter once again, she knew immediately what she must do. Returning to the main room in which she both lived and worked, she placed the letter on the back of the console piano and sat down to play. With all seriousness and grace, she measured out Beethoven's Piano Sonata no. 14 in C-sharp Minor as if she were playing at Carnegie Hall before a vast audience. At the ten minute mark, she could feel the perspiration on her upper lip as she struggled to hit every note in this difficult section of the work. After completing the entire piece without error for the first time, she stood up and faced the opposite wall and took a bow. Though no one had heard her play, she could hear resounding clapping in her head.

As the imaginary sound faded, Page whispered to herself, "Perhaps now is my time."

CHAPTER 2

With the small plastic transistor radio sitting on the kitchen counter blaring out Patsy Cline's latest hit, Page was finishing up the last of her chores around the apartment. She could hardly wait to complete the tasks and drive back to her quaint hometown of Hudson, Ohio, in her 1960 Rambler American. She'd be carrying her acceptance letter to show off to her family on a beautiful spring weekend that promised great driving weather. Twirling around the kitchen with liquid pine cleanser in one hand and a sponge in the other, she put the bottle up toward her mouth as if it were a microphone and sang along with Patsy, "I fall to pieces..."

The trip up to Hudson would take only a couple of hours, and Page was timing it just right so she'd arrive for her mother's Saturday brunch specialty of biscuits and sausage gravy. Such heavy eating wasn't her usual style. In fact, eating was pretty much a luxury these days on her limited budget. However, teaching piano lessons fifteen to twenty hours per week did enable her to keep up with her rent, utilities, gasoline, and groceries she could find on sale. But one of the many great things about going home for the weekend was that her mom would see that she didn't leave without a bag of homemade goodies. Similarly, her father, a local bank president, would always slip a five-dollar bill into her bag before she left. She could often make that stretch for over several days.

The Rambler was running beautifully, and Page was so grateful for it—last year's combination birthday and graduation gift. Though it was a no-frills vehicle, she certainly didn't take it for granted that her father had paid cash for the car the week after she got home from Wesleyan. In fact, it was last summer that she'd placed her belongings in the car and headed to Columbus to take on several piano students of various ages. Mr. Holden and her teenage brother, Jeff, had followed her in the family truck all the way with the console piano, a sleeper sofa, a small table with two chairs, and a nicked-up old dresser. And, of course, there was her box of music and books. That moving day in late June was hot and humid, though it didn't seem like work to Page, who took such pride in the little apartment...and her independence.

The drive was an easy one that morning and Page passed the time contemplating her upcoming graduate program. Excitement mixed with anxiety would best describe her feelings over the thought of being assigned a piano master from such an impressive faculty. She thought about how much further along she could move toward her desires to be a world-class pianist once she could learn under the watchful eye of someone who understood technique and the pressures of performing complex pieces.

Arriving around ten o'clock a.m., Page turned onto the long driveway of her family home, which sat on a large acre lot. Driving to the rear of the old white Greek Revival style home, she was once again struck by its classic beauty. The house was old when her parents bought it after World War II ended, at a point when they felt the need for more space with the two children. Page loved the big yard and the oak tree that held her rope swing for so many years. She felt that growing up in this stately old home near the town center made for a perfect childhood, reminding her of the Normal Rockwell paintings she'd grown up seeing on the covers of the *Saturday Evening Post* that her parents kept on the coffee table in the living room.

Jumping out of the car and bounding up the back steps to the kitchen entry, Page was once again taking in the sounds and smells of home. The rusty old spring in the wood-frame screen door rang out a second octave G-flat as it stretched upon opening. Then the scent of sweet, warm biscuits reached her, and all the comforts of home came rushing in—as did Maggie, the family's blonde cocker spaniel. With tail stump wagging, Maggie was now barking, albeit delayed due to her diminished hearing in old age. Page reached down to scratch one of Maggie's long ears, while dropping her tote bag on the kitchen table, which was surrounded by built-in, white-painted wood seating.

"Mom...Jeff...Dad...Anybody home?" yelled Page. The first response was her mother, who was ascending from the cellar carrying a jar of plum preserves up the stairs.

"Page Marie Holden, I can hear you just fine," stated her mother very matter-of-factly.

"Oh, Mom, where are Dad and Jeff?"

"They're in the barn, sweetie. I'm surprised you didn't see them when you drove up."

No sooner had Ellen Holden finished her sentence than the door spring rang out again, and the guys were entering the kitchen. With that, Page dove into her bag and pulled out the envelope while squealing, "I got in, I got in! Ohio State School of Music, here I come!"

The news got an excited "wow" from her often blasé seventeen-year-old brother. And as her mother reached for the envelope to read the contents, Bob Holden flashed his usual all-knowing dad smile saying, "I never doubted you, dear. The Lord has his timing, and this must be the year. I'm happy for you, Page."

CHAPTER 3

Another Thursday afternoon in June meant piano lessons with the twins. Page rather dreaded their appearance every week at four o'clock p.m. Their tightwad mother had even negotiated a two-for-one deal with Page to take them on—thirty minutes of instruction each for the usual one-hour fee of two dollars and fifty cents. And what was worse was that they were twice the work. As the buzzer to her apartment sounded, Page took a deep breath and let it out one side of her mouth, causing the bangs to flip away from her eye.

"Good afternoon, girls. Let's start with Jane in the driver's seat and Jenny seated quietly on my sofa. Turn to song number five, Jane." Fat chance, Page thought to herself, that Jenny would sit quietly anywhere. However, it was at least worth trying to take control of the situation from the get-go.

Thursdays were her busiest days at the piano. Page had to get up early to clean her apartment, then work with her first student by nine o'clock—a blind teenage boy who was starting to show some promise. At ten she had an undergraduate music student who attended Ohio State but actually claimed to be more interested in playing the guitar. And from one to five p.m. there were several children under age ten—including the twins. By dinnertime, Page fell back exhausted and typically didn't have much time or energy for her own practice session. In fact, she only got in one session as opposed to her usual twice daily routine, which totaled about four to six hours per day, depending on her teaching schedule.

At exactly 4:55 p.m. Page closed the beginner lesson book belonging to the twins (heaven forbid one of them would excel, causing their mother to have to pay for two books) and told the girls to gather their things to sit at her small table next to the kitchenette. Page had maintained a tradition of rewarding her younger students after each lesson with a cup of cold Kool-Aid and one small cookie or some Cracker Jack. Although it wasn't much, the twins seemed to live for this moment. Her last five minutes with them seemed like an eternity as they talked incessantly and kicked each other under the table. But she was finally able to see them out the door when their mother arrived on time this evening—for a change.

However, no sooner had Page watched through her kitchen window as the car containing the twins drove off than the door buzzed once again. Rubbing her eyes from fatigue, she made her way to the door. It was a matronly and stern-looking woman with what looked like her granddaughter at the door trying to shove a copy of *The Watchtower* into her hands. Familiar enough with Jehovah's Witnesses, and knowing she wanted nothing to do with it, Page politely rejected the publication and shut the door, but not without uttering, "I'll pray for both of you."

Alone at last after her long day, Page headed to her small kitchen to find something to eat. Taking the few slices of bread she had left and grabbing a container of tuna salad out of the refrigerator, she proceeded to make a sandwich to go with some of the grape Kool-Aid from the pitcher still sitting on the counter. Flopping down in the chair, she took intermittent bites while turning the pages of the months-old *Life* magazine she "borrowed" from the local Laundromat she visited weekly. Since she couldn't afford the movies, or even the twenty cents it took to buy the latest edition of *Life* magazine that she'd seen in the Rexall drugstore, this was about as exciting as it got. Unfortunately, the cover story was all about deep-sea fishing—not a subject Page found particularly interesting, so she stared mindlessly at the pictures while she ate.

Finishing up the sandwich, she headed back into the kitchen to find the remaining piece of a strawberry-rhubarb pie her mother had sent her home with from last weekend's visit. Page loved her mom's pies, so all day she'd been thinking about gobbling up the last bit this evening. Before sticking a fork in the pie, Page realized she'd forgotten to pray over her food—something she always did. Had she been that ungrateful that she forgot God? In that same moment, she recalled her promise to pray for the two Jehovah's Witnesses who had come knocking earlier. Putting down her fork, she folded her hands and thanked the Lord for his provision and asked him to reveal himself to the two visitors through the truth and power of his Word. Amen.

CHAPTER 4

Summer had definitely arrived, and the Midwest heat and humidity were getting to Page. She had managed to collect enough funds to purchase a small oscillating fan for the apartment, which she had pointed in the direction of the piano by day and her sleeper sofa by night. She'd found it difficult to sleep on these sultry nights and was trying to catch up on some of Ernest Hemingway's works since the news of his passing last month.

Venturing out in the stifling August sun to check the mail on this Saturday afternoon, she found a packet from Ohio State that contained her registration materials for the fall quarter. Included in the materials were items from the School of Music such as the name of her academic advisor and the date for her audition. The latter would determine which professor she would be assigned to for most of her training. All this made her day, and she quickly retreated back to the fan in the apartment to review everything in the packet. She had already spent time reviewing the thick course offerings catalog that she'd obtained by stopping by the admissions office last week. Now she just needed to get through the registration process and start thinking about that audition.

The next day being Sunday, Page was up early to walk to the United Methodist Church not far from her place, just a few blocks off of Greek Row. Early arrival was essential as earlier this summer she had applied for and been offered the job as the church accompanist. Given that some of her students were away at camp or otherwise taking the summer off from piano lessons, Page thought it might be a great way to supplement the income shortfall.

By the time she arrived for the nine a.m. service, she was already feeling like a wilted flower due to the walk in the heat and humidity. However, she felt a bit revived by the somewhat functional air conditioning in the sanctuary this morning. Sliding onto the piano bench at exactly 8:15 a.m., she was ready to accompany the meager choir for one last run through of their songs before congregants began to arrive.

Working with the choir director was proving to be a bit of a challenge after just six Sundays on the job. Vivian Backlund was a perfectionist who rarely doled out gratitude. At least this morning, the kindly widower pastor, Gil Robertson, made an appearance during practice to pray for the choir. He ended with a strong "amen" and then proceeded to thank all the members, as well as Page, for their contributions to the worship service. Page assumed Pastor Robertson knew just how hard-edged Vivian could be, and his gracious words were falling easy on the singers this morning.

By 8:50 a.m., Page was starting her prelude at the organ. Though the organ wasn't her preferred instrument, she was often moved by the swells of inspiration that resounded through the room. This morning she had people on their feet for the introit even before the pastor raised his hands to signal "all rise" to the attendees.

During the sermon each Sunday, Page took her seat in the choir loft with the singers. This morning was no different, except for a nice-looking gentleman sitting alone in the third pew on the right who kept looking at her. She tried not to return his gaze but found it a bit unnerving to be constantly averting her eyes. Instead, she stared at the pages of the open Bible that rested on her lap.

The postlude was a hymn that she had rearranged a bit to be played with more flourishes and in a different octave than the original piece. Page put her all into the last thing the people heard as they departed because she wanted them to be uplifted by the music. As it turned out, many parishioners stayed seated to hear her play out, while others were milling around after the service.

As she held the final notes to add even more dramatic flair, she looked up from the piano and once again saw the man who had his eyes fixed on her. Page hurried to gather up her music and disappeared behind the wall close to the altar that led to the holding room for performers. There were still several choir members engaged in various stages of putting away their music books and hanging up their robes. As she prepared to do the same, she saw Vivian coming toward her with an index finger in the air. Oh dear, she thought, what had she done wrong to bring Vivian's criticism this morning?

"Page, dear, I need you to come fifteen minutes early to practice this Wednesday night. Can you do that for me?" Vivian asked insistently.

"Of course, Mrs. Backlund, I'll make it by five forty-five p.m. Is there something special going on next Sunday?" inquired Page.

"Nothing special. I just need you to help me organize the choir member folders with the sheet music we'll be

using. I've already placed a copy of one of the songs into
your book just in case you want to start practicing early. It's
a rather difficult piece," indicated Vivian.

Just then Vivian's attention was drawn away to admon-
ish one of the singers about how he had disappointed her
this morning. Poor Stan Osborne—he was such a slight man
and seemed to shrink even smaller when Vivian got ahold
of him. Page sighed and made a mental note to herself to
be sure to encourage Stan during practice this week.

As she gathered her things and exited out the back door
of the church and into the parking lot, she once again noticed the handsome gentleman she'd been avoiding eye
contact with during the service. She didn't know him and
had never seen him in church before.

Walking through the crunchy gravel of the lot at a faster-
than-usual pace wasn't something she was particularly good
at, especially when the heels of her pumps sunk deeper in
some spots more than others. Though she kept her eyes
forward and didn't look toward him, she couldn't help but
wonder if he was looking at her. She didn't slow down until
she'd reached the intersection a block down from the church
where she crossed the street. Feeling it was now safe to look
back, she caught a glimpse of the man out of the corner
of her eye as he was unlocking his car parked on the street
across from the church. As she made her way home to turn
on the fan and flop down in front of it with a glass of cold
water, she secretly hoped the handsome fellow might show
up again next Sunday.

CHAPTER 5

It had been a summer of heightened racial tensions in the South, increased activity on the nuclear front, and a wall built in Berlin to keep people out. Or was it to keep people in, she wondered? Page shifted in her chair as she sat through her university orientation session this September morning. Her distracted mind darted between what the advisor was saying, what was going on in the world, and her growling stomach. She also mentally debated whether or not the new President of the United States was really as handsome as some thought and marveled at the kind of summer Mays, Aaron, and Maris were having. All this, while regretting having left that Pulitzer Prize-winning book back at the apartment.

"Just about lunchtime, so please stay with me..." pleaded the instructor. Page was just not able to stay focused, and she felt badly for the instructor who was trying desperately to hold the attention of the new graduate students. She folded her hands in front of her on the desk and tried sitting very still. That lasted about thirty seconds when she realized she needed to go the restroom. In that instant, she recalled just how much coffee she'd downed this morning.

She snapped back to attention the moment the class was dismissed with a reminder that they should use the ticket stub from their orientation folder to obtain their free cafeteria lunch and then report to their assigned room based on their degree program at one o'clock p.m. sharp. Page almost lost one of her skimmers as she dashed out of the room to head for the bathroom before getting in line for lunch in the cafeteria.

It was the afternoon session for graduate students in the School of Music that held Page's attention. This was where she got more specifics about her classes and signed up for her audition time slot for the next day. After the session, the piano students were allowed to take turns practicing at the piano in one of the rehearsal rooms. Page listened as each of the new students took their turns, thinking of them as her competition. Little did she know at that time just how much they would assist, interact with, but also be pitted against each other over the upcoming academic year.

Back in the orientation room for the wrap-up session, Page was eagerly anticipating tomorrow's audition. She'd selected an afternoon time slot knowing she wasn't much of a morning person. She was already imagining that her family back home would be praying for her at the dinner table tonight. They knew what she was up against because she'd mailed a letter in the past week to tell them about her audition date. She'd make a light dinner and try to get a good night's sleep after a couple of hours of practice tonight. With a two p.m. appointment time, she'd even be able to get in some practice before lunch tomorrow. She could already feel her nervousness creeping up—and this was just the placement audition.

CHAPTER 6

Walking across campus on a lingering summer September afternoon, Page was rehearsing each note of her selected audition piece in her head. As she entered the building, she took a deep breath and exhaled. In through the nose, out through the mouth, she performed the exercise three times. Though it didn't seem to ease her nerves, she felt it was helping to clear her head.

As she entered the music room, the student from the one forty-five time slot was just standing up to take his leave. She was close enough to hear the professor in charge indicating that her fellow student would be receiving his assigned piano master information on the first day of classes when all such information would be posted on the bulletin board in the hallway outside the music room. It made Page wonder if she hadn't shown up for this audition; wouldn't they just assign her to one of the profs anyway? Admonishing herself in her own head, she was reminded that she wanted to be assigned to one of the best teachers, so she needed to stay focused on that goal.

Handing over the index card containing her name, student identification number, and other class schedule information to the music room proctor, Page took her seat at the bench and awaited instructions. Not hearing anything for what seemed like ages, she placed her hands on the keys and was about to begin when the instructor stopped her with a curt "Young lady, did I say you should begin?" Turning to face the stern voice, she slowly took her hands from the keys and placed her arms by her side, curling her fingers around the lip of the padded portion of the bench.

Without letting her respond, the instructor announced himself. "I am Professor Gavriel Weiss. Please sit up straight and stop using the bench seat as a life raft. State your chosen piece and composer and begin."

Page straightened her back and lifted her slender fingers to the keys once again while looking down at them. Now feeling as unsure of herself as she was at her first recital at age eight, she exhaled, "Chopin's opus forty-eight, number one in C Minor." But before she could proceed, she heard the professor returning to his seat while muttering under his breath, "Nocturnes... always with the nocturnes."

With tension in her neck and shoulders, Page began to play the opus and completed it without error, before dropping her shoulders and placing her hands in her lap. As she stood up from the bench, the professor muttered again, "Thank you, Miss. That will be all. You'll find your assignment on the bulletin board outside this room on the first day of classes."

Page wanted to run out but instead maintained a brisk walking departure and her composure. Once outside the building and back in the sunny beauty, she could reflect on the four minutes of music she just played. Additionally, she had a chance to replay the exchange with the rude proctor. That was just the kind of pressure she was hoping to avoid by being assigned to an encouraging and skilled piano master.

She sent up a prayer for just that as she made her way across campus to return to the apartment.

CHAPTER 7

As it was now late September, the Ohio State Buckeyes football team would soon be playing their home opener in the Ohio Stadium against Texas Christian. Page had invited her brother to go to the game with her, and because of Jeff's good grades and having a year under his belt with his driver's license, their father had even agreed to let Jeff drive the truck by himself to Columbus and back on that Saturday. However, as Page stood in front of the bulletin board just outside the music room this Monday morning, she thought perhaps the game was the only thing she'd have to look forward to during this first week of classes. What she saw on the board was the very same index card she had handed over before her audition, now tacked up with all the others. The master teacher listed next to her name on the card was none other than the rude Professor Weiss. She wanted to turn around, walk back to her apartment, crawl into bed, and pretend this wasn't really happening.

The only good news was that not a single one of her classes this quarter was taught by the obnoxious professor, although she'd have to face him from three to forty-thirty p.m. every weekday in one of the small piano rooms of the music building. Great, she thought, he'll be tired from working all day, and he'd probably be hungry for his wife's cooking every night around that time, making him even more difficult to deal with. For a moment, she wondered if she should stop by the office of her academic advisor to see if it were possible to be reassigned to a different professor. But then she realized how that would be a cloud over her year-long program each and every time she did have to see Professor Weiss in other classes. Anyway, she knew she couldn't avoid him because he taught music theory courses that were required of her degree program. She'd just have to steel herself for his abuse. Professor Weiss was going to make Vivian Backlund seem like the sweetest thing this side of the Olentangy River.

At exactly three o'clock p.m. that same afternoon, Page knocked on the small glass insert in the door to the music room where she could see Professor Weiss staring at sheet music on the black stand next to the piano. He turned to see her there and rather than opening the door for her, he simply waved impatiently at her to enter. Once inside the small space, he commanded her to shut the door and sit at the piano. As she sat down, Weiss said nothing as he pulled up the only other chair in the room, pointing it toward her as she faced the piano. He then placed sheet music on the rack in front of her. It was the music of Chopin that she had played during her audition the day before—a piece she had selected because she thought it reflected her willingness to take on a moderately challenging composition.

The professor sat down and folded his hands in front of his face, making a steeple of index fingers that covered his lips. Page sensed that he was forcing himself not to speak or at least holding back criticism with those fingers. Yet no sooner did she find herself preparing for the potential onslaught than he dropped his hands and rapped one of them on the side of the piano. Knocking the wood three times, he inquired, "Miss Holden, what is this piano made of?"

Now completely caught off guard and knowing very little about how pianos were built, she haltingly responded with, "I'm sure I don't know, sir."

"Why don't you know, Miss Holden? Is it not your instrument of choice? You wish to be a great pianist, and yet you know nothing about your piano. You have much to learn. Now, play this piece again for me on this piano made of maple wood."

Completely discombobulated, Page straightened her back and lifted her fingers to the keys. As the piece progressed to the three-minute mark, the brown-haired and brown-eyed professor spit out the word "Stop." Leaning his six-foot frame in toward her face, he continued with, "You play this section *doppio movimento*—12/8 meter against your right hand's sixteenths. It's all wrong, and you shall owe Chopin and me an apology. I repeat—you have much to learn."

Page could feel the sting of tears coming on but refused to cry in front of this insensitive beast of a professor. She endured the remainder of her class time, with him drilling her on the same number repeatedly until she grew to hate the opus. All she could think of was how would she ever endure a full academic year of this?

CHAPTER 8

Despite the disappointing tie football game the day before, Page and Jeff had a wonderful time together. She loved her brother, who had grown to the height of five feet ten inches during his junior year, making her feel short at five feet seven. And, while they had built another great memory together as siblings, Jeff was now back home studying for his Monday morning biology test at Hudson High, and Page was back at the organ this Sunday. She couldn't help but notice that the gentleman she'd seen earlier in the summer was once again staring at her from his perch in the third row. She thought it odd that he had vanished for the summer, only to reappear in the fall. However, she put it out of her mind in order to put forth her best effort on the prelude this morning as congregants were gathering for worship.

As she moved on to the first hymn, everyone rose to sing "Come, Thou Almighty King" while the choir made their way down the aisle with Pastor Robertson following behind them. The black-robed choir reached their loft and all seemed right with the world to Page. However, when everyone had been seated for the morning announcements, Page was stunned to hear the good pastor state that his son was visiting again from Cleveland where he practiced medicine. Robertson pointed to the third row pew and had his son stand up for all to see. Now Page knew who the stranger was. Everyone clapped as the gentleman sat back down.

"John is my only child, and it's probably a good thing, too, because it took all I had of a minister's salary to get him through medical school here at Ohio State," the pastor jested. With that, Page could swear she saw some of the elders looking down at their feet over the comment. Hmmm, Page thought, that certainly explains why Vivian had warned her not to ever ask for a raise beyond her five dollars a week wage, because the church could barely afford her as it was. Not that Page had ever thought about asking for a raise. Heck, she was happy just to have any income at all now that she was no longer taking piano students due to her own educational demands. All that made her grateful for parents who were willing to pay her seventy-five dollars monthly rent and utilities, in addition to her $450 Ohio state resident tuition and fees. And even though her schooling was so much cheaper at the public university than her private school undergraduate program, Page always appreciated the sacrifice her parents were making for her dreams.

As the service ended, it didn't take Page long to get her belongings together in the back room. This time she decided she'd exit out the front door through the sanctuary in order to find the pastor to ask him for prayer. Making her way down the three rounded steps of the raised altar area into the center aisle where she could see Pastor Robertson at the front door shaking hands with parishioners, a hand reached out to grab her arm. As her eyes followed the hand upward, she was staring right into the crystal blue eyes of

Dr. John Robertson who whispered her name.

"You are Miss Holden, correct?" the doctor inquired.

"Why yes, doctor, I am," she replied.

"I wanted to introduce myself to the new organist when I was here this past summer, though you seemed to be in a hurry to get away that Sunday."

Page now felt badly that she had not been friendlier toward the gentleman and chalked it up to her introverted nature. After all, she was the gal who had captured both of Hudson High School's 1956 graduating class's seemingly incongruous superlatives categories: "Most Shy" and "Most Likely to Succeed. "

Dr. Robertson continued with, "Miss Holden, I'm wondering if you might be interested in getting some lunch with me before I head back to Cleveland this afternoon?"

This all seemed so sudden to Page, who was formulating her response when she could see her relief coming down the aisle in the form of Pastor Robertson. As the minister approached the couple with the lunch offer still hanging in the air, Page decided to quickly change the subject. "Oh... Pastor, I was just heading your way," she blurted out.

Pastor Robertson reached out to her with his kind smile, while asking her how he could help her this morning. She glanced over at the doctor, then back at the pastor, who leaned over to chide his son a bit with, "I see it didn't take you long to introduce yourself to one of the loveliest single ladies in the church, John."

With that, the doctor announced that Page was about to take him up on his offer to lunch together. A bit taken aback by the presumption, but recognizing the game, Page nodded her head and indicated to her pastor that it was now all a matter of deciding where to eat.

"Well, that's wonderful!" exclaimed Pastor Robertson. "You two have a great lunch and travel mercies on you as you return home, John." Then the pastor continued on down the aisle, leaving the couple standing in the middle of the church.

"Well, I noticed that you walked home from church last time. I have my car, so I'd be happy to take you anywhere you like and then return you to your home afterward," offered Dr. Robertson.

CHAPTER 9

The tan, tall, and well-built Dr. Robertson had been quite the gentleman throughout their lunch. In fact, it was while Page was reflecting back on their time together that her Music Composition professor called on her in class to recite some of the material from last week's instruction.

"Um, I'm sorry, sir. What was the question again?" Page stuttered. The professor wasn't even willing to repeat himself and impatiently moved on to the young lady sitting to her left for the response.

As Page exhaled out of the corner of her mouth, those bangs flipped away from her left eye. She felt like a failure this morning and was already starting to dread her afternoon class with the professor she'd begun secretly referring to as "Not-So-Nice Weiss." That's the prayer request she never got to talk to Pastor Robertson about—the professor. She needed prayer to get through these teaching sessions with such a difficult personality, while at the same time actually trying to learn something from him.

Page ducked into the music library for a quick bite of lunch between classes, but soon found her thoughts returning to her lunch date with Dr. Robertson. Per her request, he had taken her to Sandy's for hamburgers. It was just the kind of treat Page couldn't afford, so she savored every burger bite and downed every last drop of her chocolate malt.

John Robertson had certainly been polite and respectful. Page had studied his facial features, noting how much he took after his father, though he was definitely taller than the pastor. He kept his sandy blond hair short—a bit like a soldier, only without the flattop. And though she hadn't asked him, Page assumed that he was about thirty years old. In fact, he had only just completed his residency a few years earlier, so she figured he might be about that age. And while they had a good time together, she wasn't sure she'd see him again due to his busy schedule as an emergency room physician in a big urban hospital in Cleveland. Besides, she thought to herself, he probably didn't find her to be very interesting due to her shy nature. Yes, she'd tried to hold up her end of a conversation, but she felt he'd had to do most of the heavy lifting as he asked his open-ended questions in a clear attempt to get her to talk about herself. Page slumped in her chair this afternoon as she wondered to herself if she'd ever be found intriguing by any man. She wasn't even surprised that Dr. Robertson hadn't asked for her phone number or mentioned another visit to Columbus so that they might see each other again.

After racing from her previous class that afternoon, her hand reached to open the door of her music room at 3:07 p.m. Page softly entered and was immediately greeted with a terse, "You're late."

Page spoke a soft "I'm sorry." Professor Weiss pointed to the piano bench without a glance or a word. His behaviors toward her always made her feel like a puppy being trained to heel. Not willing to take it any longer, she simply remained standing and glared at the professor. Several seconds passed before he looked up from the sheet music he was working on to see that she wasn't complying with his orders. For one of the first times in their acquaintance, the two were actually looking directly in each other's eyes. The intensity was too much for Page, who was the first to look away as she moved to slip into place on the bench. So much for her standing protest, she thought to herself.

"Today we're going to work on that piece involving crossing over," explained the professor. As she placed her hands on the keys to begin the piece, he once again moved to stand behind her. Page always found this unnerving because she couldn't read his body language and facial expression to know if he approved. However, at this point, she figured that it probably didn't matter because he never seemed to approve.

As the piece progressed to the sections involving crossing over, Weiss stopped her in midcross. "No, no... You can't swing your body over the bench to do this. You look like you're reaching and uncomfortable. This needs to be and appear effortless. Do you understand?"

Page nodded and picked things up at the preceding stanza. Once again, Weiss stopped her, and Page dropped her head, shoulders, and hands and let out a sigh.

"This time you didn't swing, you swayed—it's unacceptable, Miss Holden," the professor stated in a monotone voice that clearly ignored her sigh. "Begin again, from the start of the piece," he demanded.

Page stiffened her back and her resolve while beginning again. Within seconds of her arrival at the crossing over section, she felt Professor Weiss's hands reach for her tiny waistline to hold her firmly in place. It startled Page, but she proceeded to stay in place and make the musical transitions in two locations on the sheet music before he removed his hands and stood back. Page completed more crossings and the entire piece without interruption from Weiss. As the last note sounded, he walked across the room and began to write down her homework into her assignment book.

Page just couldn't take the silent treatment and blurted out, "Well, did I do it right?"

Weiss dropped his forehead and looked down at her over his nose before responding with, "What do you think?"

"I think it was perfect!" responded Page with triumphal assurance.

The professor continued to scowl at her and came back with, "I wouldn't go that far, Miss Holden, though it was significantly better. Now, run along and continue to practice this piece. I will want you to perfect it for student recital week in the hall later this month." With that, Professor Weiss returned to staring at his notes and appeared to be done speaking, dismissing her early from class.

Page gathered up her things and departed the small practice room as quietly as she'd attempted to sneak in earlier. As she walked back across campus to her apartment, she couldn't help but think that the session was rather like when her dad held onto the seat of her bike when she was learning to ride. She recalled the feeling of exhilaration the day he let go and she sped off down the tree-lined neighborhood street on her own. Page was having that same feeling of accomplishment, though it was mixed with a strange emotion that seemed misplaced and hard to explain. Weiss had touched her, and she liked it.

CHAPTER 10

It was another stunning day in Ohio with its red, gold, and dark green foliage starting to sweep across the landscape. About halfway through the academic quarter, Page found herself preparing for her turn "in the tank" on her piano recital. The graduate piano students had their performances each week throughout the quarter, and Page was scheduled for the week of Thanksgiving. She was glad to have that date because she figured if it was awful, she could run home to Hudson for the holidays and drown her sorrows in her mom's fabulous home cooking.

In order to get in one last practice under pressure, Page had requested to play her recital number as the prelude in church this Sunday before her Tuesday performance. Vivian Backlund wasn't particularly supportive of the idea of a prelude that wasn't performed on the organ, though she had begrudgingly agreed to let Page start the service with her rehearsal piece. As Page sat down at the piano this Sunday morning, out of the corner of her eye, she saw Dr. Robertson sitting in the front row. That made her even more nervous, and she couldn't help wondering why he was in town again. Setting it aside, she took a deep breath and cleared her mind and began playing. Since it was a lengthy number, she had started five minutes earlier than usual this morning, which meant that attenders were still wandering in. As she played, people who were chatting as they entered quickly quieted down and found their seats.

Page concluded the piano number without error and was feeling quite happy with herself when Dr. Robertson stood up and began clapping. Within seconds, others were rising to their feet to do the same. Even Pastor Robertson was on his feet, clapping and smiling at Page. She felt a flush rising from her neck to her cheeks as she really didn't want to draw attention to herself during a worship service. She was grateful for the appreciation but relieved when parishioners settled back down in their seats so she could move to the organ for the choir processional.

After the service, Page did a reprise of her piano recital work, playing just the last movement. And as she stood up to collect her things and retreat to the back room with the choir members, the good doctor had already made his way to the piano to greet her.

"Page, that was an incredible performance! Was that the number you told me you were working on when we had lunch last month?" he inquired. Page could hardly recall what she was working on at the time they talked about her music over lunch.

"No, I don't think so—it's new. In fact, it's an assignment for a recital I must give at the college on Tuesday."

Dr. Robertson went on to praise her profusely and pro-ceeded to tell her he would be in town all week as he was on vacation to spend time with his father. "Hey, I'd love to attend. Is your recital open to the public, Page?" Page indicated that she wasn't exactly sure but would find out tomorrow. "Please do; I'd be happy to hear that again—and to be of moral support to you, particularly in light of that beastly professor you told me about," Dr. Robertson stated with a chuckle. "If you would provide me with your phone number, I'll give you a call tomorrow evening to see if I might attend. That is, if you're okay with my attending." Page nodded affirmatively as Dr. Robertson took out a pen and small pad from his suit jacket and handed it to her to write down the number.

This time, the doctor didn't ask her to lunch but instead said his goodbyes and retreated to the entryway where his father was shaking hands with the last of the churchgoers. Page retreated to the choir room that was almost empty now, though Vivian was still present. "That was a fine performance this morning, Page," she stated, while not even looking up from her task of arranging the choir robes on their hangers.

"Thank you, Mrs. Backlund. I only hope I can do as well during my recital on Tuesday."

"It seems that Doctor Robertson has taken an interest in your music—or more likely, an interest in you," Vivian went on to speculate out loud. Page didn't like the way the conversation was going, so she quickly gathered her things and headed for the back door with an "I'm sure it's the music—have a good week, Mrs. Backlund."

CHAPTER 11

Tuesday had arrived after Monday's difficult class session in the small practice room. Professor Weiss had been hard on Page, and now there he was glaring at the piano from his front-row seat in the recital hall. Page and another student performing on this afternoon had pulled back the heavy, blue drape to peer into the hall that was built in the round. The glossy black Steinway was on a raised platform in the center of the room, so the performer only had to maneuver two steps and walk onto the stage to sit down at the piano bench.

Page's nerves were evident as she fidgeted with her bra strap under the white shell top she was wearing. All the students were instructed to wear only black and white, and Page's mother had made sure she had the classic full-length, black skirt for such events. The only adornment Page had added to the plain outfit was a delicate gold cross necklace she'd received as a high school graduation gift from her parents.

On her tiptoes and peering over Page's shoulder was Alison Blake, who was searching the audience for her father, a government employee in Columbus. Alison was whining about not being sure he'd be able to get away from the office for a midday recital. That just served to remind Page of the fact that Dr. Robertson had promised to be in the audience. Just as the thought came to her, she heard one of the music professors announce her name. That was her cue; she would be the first to perform. This was her moment to shine.

Ever so conscious of her stride, posture, and the potential for her heel to catch the hem of her long skirt, she carefully made her way to the platform and sat down at the piano. The room was silent as she placed her hands on the keys and began to play. Everything Professor Weiss had taught her was ringing in her ears. She didn't sway, she didn't reach, she didn't look down at her hands during the crossing-over portions, but she also didn't reach one of her high notes with enough vigor to make it audible. With one mistake made, she prayed silently for no others. As the minutes that seemed like hours drew to a close, Page finished strong. As instructed, she stood up and took a bow to the tepid applause, which she knew was ginned up by classmates to help spur each other onward. Now she couldn't make it off this stage fast enough and hide behind the cover of the billowy, blue drapes. Passing Alison, who was making her way toward the steps, Page didn't even make eye contact. She just kept walking out the back and through the doors to the outer hallway where she stopped and leaned up against the wall. Though she'd made it through the piece without serious problems, she knew it wouldn't cut it with her mentor. She snorted at the word when it came to her mind. Some mentor he'd turned out to be. Weiss was certainly a gifted pianist, but he hardly had an encouraging word for her—even on her best days.

Just as she raised her head, she saw Dr. Robertson coming her way with his hand outstretched. She knew she'd have to pull her hands from behind her back to meet his. While shaking her hand, the kind doctor was carrying on about how well she'd performed. All she could think of was how easy it was to fool the layman when it came to such things. However, she knew she'd have to be a good sport, so she accompanied him back into the recital hall to sit in the last row of seats to listen to the rest of the student performances. This was not only expected, but something the graduate students had verbally promised to do for each other throughout this year: support and encourage.

As the last graduate student concluded his presentation and was seated, Professor Weiss rose to speak. The acoustics in the room were excellent, and in that moment, the silence was deafening. Finally, he spoke, "Thank you all for your participation, and thanks to our community guests for coming today. Students, your grades will be posted after you return from the Thanksgiving holiday, and we'll do this again next quarter—as we do every quarter...until you all get it right." There was nervous laughter about the room because most weren't even sure that Professor Weiss had a sense of humor.

CHAPTER 12

Dr. Robertson was insisting on taking Page to dinner after the recital, despite her arguments about needing to do some last-minute studying for her midterm exam the next day. "You've got to eat, Page. Allow me to share a bite with you before you head back to hit the books," said the doctor. He opened the car door for her and then walked quickly around to the driver's side. Once inside the car, he reached down to fish something out from under his seat. Coming up with a small box of chocolates, he presented it to Page with a hearty "Congratulations!"

"Thank you very much, Doctor. You really shouldn't have. After all, it was just a recital, and I think my better performance was last Sunday in church anyway."

But the doctor wouldn't hear of it. "Page, you were wonderful, and please feel free to call me John. I think we can dispense with the formalities. I want you to know that I really enjoy your company and was hoping you might even consider spending some time with me over the holiday."

Page felt badly to have to explain that she was driving home for the holidays and would only be able to see him in church on Sunday when she was due back to play. However, they did agree to have lunch again after church and before John had to make the drive back to Cleveland.

John Robertson parked his 1958 red Bel Air in front of the Ohio Union where the two became better acquainted over their early bird dinner in the cafeteria. Page discovered that she'd guessed John's age exactly. She also learned more about the passing of his mother about twelve years earlier from breast cancer.

He went on to explain, "Actually, it was my mother's medical struggles in the last year of her life that caused me to enter Ohio State as a premed student in biology. I spent lots of time at her bedside in the last two months of her illness, paying particular attention to what the physicians were saying about her case. I really miss her a great deal, and I'm not sure my father has ever been quite the same for the loss."

"I'm sorry for your loss, John. I know how much I rely on my mother for advice and counsel. I'd miss my mother terribly too. But are you glad you went into medicine after all?"

"Oh yes, I thoroughly enjoy my work, especially glad I chose the fast-pace of emergency medicine. I think it suits my personality. I'm just a natural responder under pressure. Though I must say, I don't think I could take the kind of pressure you deal with in performing in such a public way. Do you like that?"

Page thought for a moment about how much her music carried her away such that an audience became secondary. "Yep. Though when I feel the pressure of performing, it's likely I'm not playing as well in those moments. I'm afraid I felt a bit that way at today's recital. I feel like I do my best when I get lost in the music—my first love."

After an enjoyable meal together, John reached for Page's jacket to hold it for her as she slipped her arms within. As the two walked out into the crisp fall late afternoon and as he began to escort her to his car, Page was once again feeling sorry for herself over the performance. She stopped abruptly at the sidewalk and informed John that she'd prefer to walk back to her apartment... alone. Though he began to argue with her, she interrupted him by thanking him again for the meal and wishing him a wonderful Thanksgiving. She also followed up with, "I look forward to seeing you in church after the holiday." With that, Page turned to walk home alone.

"Sure, Page, I'll see you then," John said quietly as he watched her walk away.

Once Page arrived at her apartment, she placed her jacket and the chocolates on the back of the piano and sat down. She played through her recital piece without error this time, then pounded her fists on the piano bench when she was done. The old adage of crying over spilt milk came to mind, and she mentally acknowledged she was overreacting. But the disappointment she felt wasn't mental, it was emotional. Besides, she was also physically exhausted. Furthermore, she dreaded hearing more about her failures from Professor Weiss when she returned from the holiday.

CHAPTER 13

The midterm exams were a breeze for Page, so she was feeling pretty confident as she jumped in her car on Wednesday afternoon to begin the drive home to Hudson. In fact, the only grade she was concerned about was the one she'd have to see posted upon her return to campus next Monday. But for now, she was looking forward to a few days with her family.

Those days passed quickly as she and her brother spent time helping their father with some fall cleanup around the property. Of course, much of that involved Jeff pushing Page into the piles of leaves they had raked, all the while reminding her that spiders were in those piles. Jeff knew all of her worst fears and pet peeves, as brothers often do... and take advantage of.

Page also enjoyed peeling the potatoes for her mother in preparation for the wonderful mashed potatoes and turkey gravy she'd enjoy that Thanksgiving. Mrs. Holden and her daughter had an easy relationship, so it wasn't long into the kitchen chores before Page mentioned to her mom that she'd gone to lunch a couple of times with the pastor's son down in Columbus. Ellen Holden raised an eyebrow as she continued kneading her county-fair-winning pie crust dough.

"What do you think of him, Page?"

"Oh, he's very nice—nice looking too. And I suppose it doesn't hurt that he's a medical doctor," responded Page as she turned to check her mother's reaction to the summary.

Balling up the dough to put in the refrigerator, Mrs. Holden responded, "No, I suppose none of that hurts. However, I encourage you to stay focused on your studies, dear. Remember, you still have a long road ahead of you to finish this degree program that you worked so hard to get into."

As Page tossed the last bits of potato into the large pot on the kitchen counter, she used her forearm to move her bangs away from her eyes and attempted to put the strands of hair behind her ear. "I know, Mom. It's just that I'm already discouraged, and it's only the first quarter."

"What's that all about, Page?"

"It's about the piano professor I've been assigned to. Oh, Mom, he's just cranky, mean, and unforgiving. Every day I go to the music room and dread opening the door because I know those ninety minutes are going to be nothing but awful."

Just as she finished her sentence, Bob and Jeff Holden came in the kitchen door laughing and joking about the neighbors having duck for Thanksgiving this year. Page just glared at them because she knew the Slater family raised several ducks on their property. In fact, it was Page who had pulled one of those ducks from Maggie's soft mouth several years ago and saved its little life.

"I don't want to hear another word about it, you two," stated Mrs. Holden sternly because she could see it had upset Page. Though Page also overheard her dad whisper under his breath as he walked through the kitchen, "Now, Mother, they aren't pets, you know."

Despite the news of duck dinner next door, the Holden family had a quiet holiday filled with goodies, board games, and even watching the new television show Mrs. Holden had gotten hooked on this season—*Dr. Kildare*. Page found the program somewhat intriguing, and it made her wonder more about Dr. Robertson's job up in Cleveland. She even found herself wondering how he and his father were doing this Thanksgiving. Then her mind jumped to a scene of Professor Weiss criticizing his wife's cooking over their dinner table. Oh, that poor woman, she thought to herself.

Page got back in her car on Saturday night to drive back to Columbus pretty late that evening. In fact, it was already dark and her parents were sitting down in the living room to watch the *Perry Mason* show when she kissed them goodbye and thanked them for a wonderful holiday. As she backed the car down the long lane to the street, she caught a glimpse of Maggie standing on her hind legs at the front picture window. Page waved to Maggie, even though she figured her beloved dog's eyesight was probably too poor to see her do so.

CHAPTER 14

Musically speaking, things went well at the church on Sunday, and as Page lifted her feet from the organ pedals to slip off the bench at the end of the service, she could already see Dr. Robertson heading up the steps toward her in the front of the church. She was looking forward to their lunch together, and John appeared to be feeling the same.

"That was lovely, Page. Are you hungry?" he asked with expectancy in his voice.

"Sure am!" responded Page as she proceeded to tell him she'd meet him in the foyer after heading to the music room in back.

Once the two had met up and said their goodbyes to Pastor Robertson, they hit the cold, damp air outside. They both agreed that they could feel the gray of winter starting to overtake the colorful, sunny days of fall. Heading to a nearby eatery on High Street, the couple talked about how they spent their holidays. Page even got up the nerve to ask John what he thought of the new *Dr. Kildare* television show. John just smirked and told Page he'd watched the first episode and hadn't found it to be very realistic. He did go on to say that he could see why it might be a hit with the ladies since the actor who played Kildare was thought to be a handsome fellow. For a moment, Page wondered if perhaps John was fishing for a compliment right then and there. However, she didn't bite and quickly changed the subject.

"Tell me what it was like being raised as a PK," prompted Page. With that inquiry, John proceeded to launch into a bit of a diatribe about the woes of being a preacher's kid.

"Oh, the usual—church two to three times a week, plenty of awful potluck food, having to help out with vacation Bible school every summer, and trying not to doze off during sermons."

Page assumed these were the normal complaints from a child's perspective on their parental profession, until John's attitude seemed to shift to one with an edge to it.

"Don't get me wrong, Page; I love my parents. I've just never bought into all the God-talk. I understand why having some kind of faith works for people. I even see it in my work. People with a faith belief of any type do tend to heal better. However, as a man of science, I know it's just mind over matter at play."

Page sat back in her booth as the conversation unfolded. She could hardly imagine that John believed what he was saying. She finally tilted her head to the side and asked him, "Then why the charade, because it appears your father thinks you are a believer?"

"It's not a charade, Page. My father knows where I stand. He just keeps on telling me he's praying for me," the doctor said with a bit of a forced smile.

"Well, I will be praying for you too," stated Page before she even thought about how her statement might be received. But John didn't seem to be fazed by her declaration.

He reached over and patted her hand on the table and quietly said, "If it makes you feel better, please do."

The whole conversation caused Page to realize that she really didn't know much about John Robertson at all. And though she didn't dare ask, she wondered if his mother had known where he stood—or had she passed away never having assurance of her son's future in heaven with her? The whole thing made her sad enough to announce that she'd better be getting back to her apartment to prepare for the week ahead. John obliged, but as he dropped her off at her place, he reached for her hand and kissed it before letting her step out of the car.

As she opened her apartment door and then shut it behind her, Page stood quietly for a few moments before taking off her coat. It was in those few moments that she asked God to send the Hound of Heaven to track down John's soul.

CHAPTER 15

Another Monday afternoon and Page placed her hand on the doorknob of the piano room while sending up a prayer that things would go better than she was expecting. Peering through the small glass window in the door, she could see Professor Weiss sitting on the chair in the room marking up some sheet music. As she entered, he didn't even look at her or speak, so Page took off her overcoat and placed it and her satchel on the wall hook near the bench seat and sat down at the piano. She looked straight ahead and matched his silence.

After what seemed like an endless space of time, Weiss stood up and approached the piano. She sensed that he might be looking at her, but she wasn't willing to make eye contact. Out of the silence came a question: "You were wearing that gold cross at the recital, weren't you, Miss Holden?"

Startled, Page looked up and directly into his dark brown eyes. "Why, yes, I guess I was, Professor."

"Why do you wear it?"

"It was a gift from my parents, and it represents my faith," she responded, still looking directly into his eyes.

"So, you're a Christian then?" Weiss inquired in a statement kind of way.

Without hesitation, Page responded, "Yes, I am." And as she continued to make direct eye contact with him, she asked, "Are you?"

Weiss seemed unable to continue looking at her any longer and turned to walk around the piano to stare out the window instead. Page's own brown eyes followed his movements around the room as she noticed his casually rumpled, mud-colored pants and his camel-colored corduroy jacket, which sported dark leather patches at the elbows.

"No, Miss Holden, I wear a gold Star of David, though not openly. It was a gift from my parents as well, and I am Jewish. In a world still dealing with anti-Jewish sentiment, I don't feel as free to show mine off as you do yours."

"Why not? You should feel just as free to do so. Though I like my necklace because it's pretty, I wear mine outwardly because my faith means a great deal to me. Isn't it the same for you?"

"No, Miss Holden, it is not the same for me. However, I wear it because it was a gift from my mother," responded Weiss as he turned to face her again. But he appeared agitated this time, so Page was not sure she should continue the conversation. And just as she was contemplating what to say next, he pointed his finger at her and, in a slightly raised voice, declared, "You missed a note at the recital. I couldn't hear that B-flat at all, Miss Holden. What went wrong?"

Page was crestfallen, though not surprised that the professor would start the lesson on what was quite literally a bad note. She attempted to regain his gaze, but he moved around the piano and returned to his seat as she responded.

"I just didn't hit it hard enough; my finger simply brushed it due to the speed of those measures."

Weiss never looked up at her and simply demanded that she play the number correctly for him. Page sat up straight and began to play. Just a few notes into the piece, he abruptly stood up and shouted, "Attack!" Page just dropped her hands to her lap in confusion. Professor Weiss seemed equally confused. "Why aren't you attacking this piece, Miss Holden? It's the only way you can be assured of not missing a single note."

Page could feel tears starting to well up in her eyes as she blurted out, "Because I'm afraid to play in front of you and your critical spirit." At that point, the tears seemed to leap from her eyes, and she felt forced to gather up her belongings and run out of the room.

CHAPTER 16

Page was secretly rejoicing to see the note on the music room door for the next three consecutive days: Class Cancelled—Professor Weiss Out Ill. Each one of the days seemed to be a shelter in the storm to her.

On Tuesday, she spent the time studying in the music library with a few of her fellow students, after which they headed to the student union for some burgers, fries, and shakes. Though Page could only afford the fries, the friends each contributed some of their milkshakes to an empty glass to make a complete one for her.

On Wednesday, she saw the note on the door and practically skipped off the campus at two p.m. to flop on her sleeper sofa for an afternoon nap before heading to the church for choir practice. Things were getting very busy as the Christmas season was approaching, so she was glad to have the rest prior to the longer-than-usual practice session that Vivian held that night. Trudging home in the dark and cold that night, she hoped that the note would be there again tomorrow. In her mind, she imagined Mrs. Weiss having her chicken soup rejected by a sick and surly husband at home.

On Thursday, she saw the note again and actually began to feel sorry for the professor—but not too much. She spent the three o'clock hour in one of the practice rooms with Alison, who had asked for Page's help on a difficult piece she was trying to master, but still managed to get home before dark.

Opening a can of spinach to go with a cold leftover chicken leg she had in the fridge, Page sat at her little kitchen table while the vegetables were heating up in the saucepan. This was her big chance to read the *Life* magazine from the end of November that she'd swiped from her trip home for Thanksgiving. The cover story was about the nursery at the White House, with little John-John Kennedy featured on the front. But before she opened the magazine, she thought she'd pray over her meal even before it was ready. With the spinach starting to steam in the background, Page bowed her head to pray, audibly this time. "Lord, thank you for my food—as meager as it is. I know you've promised to take care of me, and I acknowledge that you always do. Please take care of my family back home too. Also, I continue to ask your Spirit to draw John Robertson to yourself. Amen...uh...and please take care of Professor Weiss by making him well. Amen."

As she raised her head, she realized it was the first time she'd prayed for the professor—and not just in the sense of asking the Lord to help her bear up under his pressure. No, she heard herself pray for him specifically. And because Page believed in the power of prayer, she knew in that moment that she'd be returning to his classroom tomorrow.

Sure enough, Professor Weiss was back at it the next day and for the last few weeks of the quarter before Christmas break. And the mood on campus was just about as sour as his due to the Faculty Council decision to disallow the undefeated Buckeyes football team to go to the Rose Bowl in January. Word was apparently out in the local papers about who sat on the Council and which faculty members voted no. Page wasn't paying much attention to the student demonstrations or the taunting of the faculty, so she wasn't even sure if Weiss was on the Council and might be dealing with that problem as well.

In an attempt to try to make things a bit better for him, Page even wished him a happy Hanukkah during the first week in December, though he only grunted at the nicety. And though he never mentioned her outburst and dramatic exit from the classroom before his illness, he also never spoke of anything personal again that quarter. However, he did wish her safe travels home and a good holiday on her last day of class. She even felt comfortable enough to tell him that she would be driving back to Columbus for a seven p.m. Christmas Eve service at the Methodist church and then back home again that night, so she was just praying it would not be a white Christmas. He complimented her on supplementing her music experience with the job and wished her a good performance.

Unfortunately, it did start snowing on the morning of the day before Christmas Eve, so Page never made it to the church due to the road conditions and travel warnings all over the state of Ohio. Vivian Backlund took her place for that sparsely attended Christmas Eve service. When Page arrived back in Columbus after the holidays, Vivian registered her displeasure but also couldn't resist telling her that she'd overheard Dr. Robertson asking about her.

CHAPTER 17

Winter quarter brought new classes, and though she still had her sessions with Professor Weiss, they were now scheduled for nine a.m. Page was hoping he'd be in a better mood in the mornings, but it didn't seem to work that way. On one particular day, he even walked out on her playing. Page sat in the room and practiced until ten, but the professor never returned.

With her heavy academic load, the discouragement she felt under Professor Weiss's tutelage, and the dark winter weather, it ended up being quite a difficult quarter for Page. The bright spots were the few times that Dr. Robertson would call or show up in town for the weekend. The two had become good friends, even though Page sensed that the doctor was hoping for something more.

But toward the end of the quarter, she was starting to gear up for her favorite season in the Church—Easter! Page loved the music of the season and would even be taking part in accompanying the university choir for some of their performances of Handel's *Messiah*. Even her winter recital performance had gone much better because she'd done so much practicing in and out of school.

And it was on a day during the last week before final exams that Page showed up ten minutes early for her morning class with Professor Weiss when she walked by the large recital hall and heard beautiful music coming from inside. She stuck her head in the open door only to see Professor Weiss at the piano. Page decided to stay hidden in the shadows near the door but entered to listen. Weiss appeared so intense in his playing, so brilliant, so animated, and so perfect in his delivery. Once she got past the execution, she studied the pianist. He seemed completely relaxed as his long fingers caressed the keys. Almost without effort, he was able to bend the will of the instrument to his. But there was something else Page noticed about Gavriel Weiss. He was an amazing specimen of a man. Though it was deathly cold outside, he had removed his jacket and played in a short sleeve shirt. The muscles in his arms defined themselves as he played. He had a handsome and smooth olive skin tone, and when she closed her eyes, she could visualize his brown eyes. When she opened her eyes again at the crescendo of the arrangement he was playing, she noticed that a strand of his longish brown hair fell over one eye. Given her own problem with that, it made her snigger, and he stopped cold in the middle of his playing. Before he could locate the muffled sound, Page jumped out of the room and began briskly walking to her classroom. She was embarrassed that she'd made a noise but was pretty confident he never saw her.

Page was already seated at her piano bench with her sheet music before her when Professor Weiss entered the practice room. He seemed a bit flustered, so she didn't make eye contact. Before beginning their session, Professor Weiss announced to Page that he'd been practicing a great deal lately for an accompaniment he was looking forward to in early May. In fact, he told her that he'd engaged a university bus to take the piano grad students up to Cleveland to hear the concert.

Page was excited about news of a field trip. Immediately, she jumped in to inquire about what and where he'd be playing. She was thrilled to find out that her own professor would be playing at Severance Hall and accompanying the brilliant violinist Jascha Heifetz for a single performance of violin and piano works of Mozart.

"Oh, Professor, what an honor that you've been selected for this," offered Page. "And to think, we get to go hear the concert too!"

"I am honored, Miss Holden. But more importantly, I am practicing for what must be excellence, which is what Heifetz demands of himself."

His stern demeanor had kicked in again, but it didn't seem to stop Page's exuberance as she blurted out, "Hey, maybe I could handle your sheet music while you play?"

Professor Weiss leaned down toward her face, looked her in the eyes, and coldly stated, "Miss Holden, that won't be necessary as you aren't even qualified to be my page turner."

CHAPTER 18

During the Passion Week, Page had several services to accompany at the church. There was a midweek service, a Good Friday service, and two services on Easter Sunday itself due to higher attendance than any other service during the year. Pastor Robertson confided in Page that as much as he appreciated the Christmas and Easter attenders as it might be the only time they heard the gospel, it always bothered him to know that many came for the wrong reasons. When he mentioned this to Page, she couldn't help but wonder how it made him feel to know his own son would be in the audience just to please his father. That thought made her sad, and she vowed to pray even more for John Robertson to have ears to hear the word of God during these services.

With all the church involvement, Page wasn't able to get home for Easter, but she was able to spend several days at home prior to the Holy Week. It was great to see Jeff now getting excited for varsity spring track and field at the high school after having lettered in cross country in the fall. Jeff loved all kinds of sports but was strongest in long distance running events. Mom and Dad were also doing well, and the whole family went out for dinner to a fancy restaurant to celebrate her parents' twenty-sixth wedding anniversary and Bob Holden having received a raise at the bank. And, of course, the family was gearing up for their own Easter services at their home church in Hudson.

The visit home to Hudson also brought an interesting possibility when Page's high school friend Jean called to let her know that there might be an opening in the Columbus school district for a high school music teacher. It was all rather hush-hush because Jean knew someone who had already signed a second-year contract for the position, but that someone was thinking of backing out by July 1 if she was accepted into the Peace Corps. Page asked Jean to keep her informed because she was already behind on her post-graduation planning. Besides, Page knew she couldn't return to the meager income provided by teaching privately.

On the day Page had to return to Columbus, the weather had decided to be very cooperative. In fact, it was almost like an early summer tease with the sunny and nearly seventy-degree day she got for the drive back to Ohio State. As she made her way there, her thoughts turned to how cruelly Professor Weiss had spoken to her when she had expressed her excitement about the trip to Cleveland. She thought, too, about how hard it had been to pray for him after that comment. She knew she should—after all, he'd be celebrating Passover soon. Or would he? Page wondered if he even thought about God during the Jewish holidays, for Weiss seemed so secular in his perspective. But yet, he wore that Star of David around his neck, though she'd never actually seen anything but the gold chain that would occasionally peek out from the V in his sweater or shirt. She knew it must mean something to him because it lay so close to his heart all the time. But feeling her fingers tightening around the steering wheel, she actually wondered out loud if he might not have a heart at all.

The Good Friday services went smoothly, and Page thought the pastor had delivered such a moving message on the Lamb of God who bore the sins of the world in his body that awful day almost two thousand years ago on a desolate and detestable hillside. How could Dr. Robertson not see his own sinful nature and his need for the free gift of forgiveness that came in the substitutionary death and glorious resurrection of Jesus Christ? And yet, seemingly unmoved, he greeted Page after the service and offered to drive her home. On the way, he asked if he might take her to lunch with his father after services on Easter Sunday. Page agreed to go with the two men and was happy to have an invitation to spend Easter with someone she knew.

As Page got out of the car to walk to her apartment door, John put the car in park and got out to walk with her this time. He seemed unfazed by the seriousness of the service they had just attended—almost jaunty in his step. He then completely surprised her by grabbing her hand and pulling her to himself as they stood on the welcome mat outside her door. Without warning, John Robertson planted a kiss on Page's lips and then turned to walk back to his car without a word.

The whole thing happened all so quickly that it wasn't until Page got into her apartment that she realized what just occurred. He hadn't so much as asked her if he could kiss her—and he apparently didn't even seem to think he should. Page wasn't sure if he was being arrogant or awkward with respect to the whole thing. However, she was now absolutely certain he was interested in advancing the relationship.

CHAPTER 19

Friday, May 4 was a gorgeous spring morning with chalky white cloud wisps high in the sky. The sun was brilliant as Page climbed aboard the bus with the other piano students. She ended up sitting near the middle of the bus next to the window. As the students found their seats for the drive to Cleveland, one of the last boarders was an international student in the graduate program, Jun Lew. He ended up sitting down next to Page, and they struck up a conversation right away, despite Jun's scrambled-up English. Jun was a gifted pianist, and Page was glad to get a few pointers from him on the way north. It was about halfway through the trip that Page learned from Jun that he'd been asked to be the page turner for Professor Weiss this evening. While she congratulated Jun, it privately took her back to that miserable day when the professor had spoken so harshly to her.

The trip took about two and a half hours, and the students were let off the bus in the pull-through driveway in front of the performing arts center where they were met by Dr. Weiss, who had already arrived in Cleveland the night before. As the group gathered around the professor, he reminded them that the performance wasn't starting until seven p.m. so they had plenty of time to tour the great hall, the Case Western campus, the art museum, or other sites. Then they were to meet across from Severance Hall about two hours before the performance for a group dinner paid for by the university. Their seating for the concert was as one block, and they could pick up tickets right after the dinner, which the professor had already indicated he would not be attending with them.

Page was so excited about visiting the area, even though she knew it would be a long day since the bus would not arrive back in Columbus until about midnight. She caught up with Alison Blake and Peggy Johnston as the three had already made plans to walk around the campus and then take in the Cleveland Museum of Art. The good news was that they could get into the museum for free by showing their student identification cards, meaning they could save their money for lunch.

After a very full day in Cleveland, the three ladies were more than ready to sit down to dinner with the rest of the students at a local restaurant that evening. Page had stuffed a pair of heels into her large tote bag so she could wear flats for all the daytime walking. Holding onto Alison's shoulder for balance, she took off her flats and slipped on the heels before entering the restaurant. When they got inside, they could hear the chatter of the student group coming from a back room of the establishment as the host directed them to the room. The three ladies were seated and about to place their orders with all the other students when the host returned to the room in a bit of a panic.

Frantically, he inquired, "Is there a student by the name of Page Holden here?" So used to raising her hand as if she were in class, Page waved at the host who came over to her side. He handed her a message he had written down word-for-word saying the gentleman who phoned it in had indicated that it was urgent. Page unfolded the half sheet to read the scrawled handwriting:

> Mr. Lew has taken ill from something he ate this afternoon off campus. That leaves me with no page turner for this evening's performance. Since you offered to assist last month, I would ask that you come to my aid. Please forgo the dinner and make your way to Severance Hall. Pick up your ticket at the window and proceed to the orchestra area. Someone there will bring you to me.
>
> Expect to see you shortly,
>
> Weiss

Stunned, thrilled, and scared was what Page felt in that moment. And, though she was hungry, all thoughts of food vanished as she picked up her bag and whispered to her friends that she'd have to depart because of what she'd just learned. Alison and Peggy were congratulating her as she stood up, but Page wasn't listening much while dashing out of the restaurant and heading toward the great hall as fast as her heels would carry her.

Chapter 20

The first-chair cellist in the orchestra seemed relieved to make Page's acquaintance as she pointed toward an exit door where Page would find Dr. Weiss in the second room on the right. Page quickly made her way there and knocked on the closed door. She vaguely made out Dr. Weiss's voice saying, "Come in." Letting herself in ever so slowly, she jumped when he raised his voice saying, "Stop skulking around and get in here."

As Page entered the small dressing room, she realized that the two were alone and suddenly felt uncomfortable in the close quarters. Thankfully, Dr. Weiss had his music book in order and handed the entire thing to her saying they should go to the stage immediately to run through the process and the music together. The two exited through a backstage door on the other side of the dressing room where they encountered a few short stairs to the door that led to the stage. Following Dr. Weiss, whose pace was so hurried that he took the steps two at a time, Page kept up, even though she could feel her heart pounding already at the thought of being on this magnificent, deeply recessed, and beautifully appointed stage with such incredible talent.

Seated slightly behind and to the left of the professor, Page moved with him through all the pages, timing, and cues. When Dr. Weiss seemed comfortable enough with Page's familiarity with the process, he looked at her as they stood up. As she stood there in her cornflower blue and white plaid shift dress with a white cardigan sweater buttoned at the top, the professor looked her up and down. Finally, he spoke up saying, "You're not exactly dressed for this part—that outfit is a bit flashy for this work. I recommend you see the costume shop to find something simple and black." Page understood the need to have this role fade into the background, but she couldn't help but wonder if the professor's commentary on one of her favorite dresses was also a reflection of disdain for her.

Finding a suitable black dress also meant temporarily discarding the white heels she was wearing for black patent pumps that didn't fit all that well. After Page put on a tea-length dress with a black silk bow at the waistline in front, the assistant dashed some rouge on her cheeks and applied some light lipstick to her lips. It was already time to take her place on stage in a black wooden folding chair hidden behind the grand piano. She would not make an entrance with Dr. Weiss but instead wait for him to be seated before moving the chair into place for the program.

As Page walked up the stairs and walked through the door to the stage, the curtains were not yet open, though she could see a young man on the other side of the stage preparing to draw them back. As she found her seat behind the gorgeous black Steinway, her heart was pounding in her chest. Near panic, she took three deep breaths and looked straight ahead to the door of the stage which she entered. As she sent up a prayer for calm and clear thinking, the curtains were drawn, and the full house of an audience began clapping in anticipation of the violin master who was about to perform for them.

Page could see Dr. Weiss emerging from the stage door when she heard the announcer tell the audience that flash photography was strictly prohibited. His rich voice then proceeded to state, "Tonight's accompanist at the piano is Dr. Gavriel Weiss, professor of piano at Ohio State University. He is assisted by one of his current graduate students."

In his black tuxedo, silver cummerbund, crisp white shirt, and black bow tie, the professor strode halfway across the stage to the front where he took one bow from the waist, while the audience clapped politely. As he made his way to the piano bench, Page moved her chair into position. At no point did Dr. Weiss look at Page, but she certainly took note of his intense focus as he opened his black music binder to the first piece.

The announcer then began to introduce Jascha Heifetz, and the audience went wild with applause as the violinist walked out onto the stage, standing to the front but slightly left of the professor. Page was awestruck to see that he carried no music with him—only his beautiful instrument. As Heifetz took several bows, the crowd continued their applause. Both Page and Dr. Weiss clapped from their seated position. Then the master began to play, and Dr. Weiss entered in with exacting precision after a brief violin prelude.

CHAPTER 21

Page was still on cloud nine as she returned to the costume area to change back into her own clothes. Her heart thrilled at what she had just seen and heard. Heifetz was brilliant, the professor was perfection, and she completed her assignment without error. In fact, both men shook her hand and thanked her once they all exited the stage and before departing for their respective dressing rooms. Page could hardly wait to get on the bus to tell her classmates all about it.

Finding her way around the maze of back hallways, Page finally spilled out into the large lobby of the beautiful neo-classic building with its stunning art deco interior. As she made her way through the crowd still milling about, she heard someone call her name. Looking toward the center of the crowd, she could see Dr. Robertson waving as he was making his way over to her.

"Page Holden, I am so proud of you!" exclaimed the doctor as he reached her side.

"Why, I didn't know you were coming tonight, John."

"This is my backyard, Page, and I really do have an appreciation for music. And who wouldn't want to come hear the incomparable Jascha Heifetz? But then, to my surprise, I get a bonus for coming tonight by seeing your loveliness up on that stage. How did you pull that off with this professor, who you tell me is so grumpy and doesn't seem to like you?" inquired John.

"Oh, John, that was an amazing turn of events. Believe me, I wasn't the professor's first choice. That student came down ill, and the professor picked me for the job at the last minute!"

"Well, congratulations. You sure prettied up that stage tonight!" John said with a smile so wide that his dimples showed. "Hey, how are you getting home from here? Are you staying someplace local that I can drive you to?" asked John as he slipped his arm around her shoulder.

Just as Page was about to respond, out of the corner of her eye she noticed Professor Weiss heading for the front doors at a brisk pace, though he didn't appear to see her. "No, thank you. Actually, I need to catch the bus back to Columbus tonight with the rest of the students," explained Page as she looked back at the doctor.

"Well, it's a shame that you aren't spending time in Cleveland this weekend. However, I'll give you a call about my next trip to Columbus so we can make plans to get together again," John announced as the crowd in the lobby was starting to thin. With that, he drew Page even closer to his body. Thinking she might miss the bus, Page pulled away, said her goodbyes, and headed outside to the front steps of the hall. The large cluster of lanterns on either side of the wide stairway were glowing gold on this clear spring night, and Page was taking care getting down the many steps in her high heels.

It was now just after nine, and the bus driver had accounted for everyone except Jun Lew, who had been admit-

ted to a local hospital with acute gastroenteritis that afternoon. The driver glared at Page as she was the last one to get
on the bus. Once seated, she was promptly pummeled with
questions from her classmates, who wanted to know what
it was like on stage and whether or not she got to meet the
violin master. Hours later as the bus pulled into the campus
entrance and dropped off the students, the excitement was
still very present for Page. So much so, that it wasn't until
she arrived back in her apartment after midnight that she
realized her stomach was growling terribly.

Dropping her bag on the table, she began hunting for
anything she could find in the cupboard. Diving for a can
of split pea soup, she turned on the stove and plopped the
mush into the saucepan with some water and began stirring.
Checking the refrigerator, she located a small bit of leftover
Waldorf salad that she loved. Adding some saltines, she was
ready to call it a meal.

Finally, sitting down to eat her belated dinner, Page took
a moment to bow her head and pray. "Lord, today was an
unexpected gift. Thank you for giving me this opportunity
and for sustaining me throughout the task. And thank you
for prompting Professor Weiss to ask me to assist. I pray you
might make this experience the basis for a better working
relationship between us going forward. I also pray for a
speedy and complete recovery for Jun Lew. Thank you for
this food. Amen."

CHAPTER 22

With just another three weeks of school remaining, Page returned to her morning classes, including her first session with Weiss since the concert in Cleveland. As she turned the corner for that class, she noticed the door was open today. She was determined not to gush over how well the professor had performed, and she certainly wasn't expecting anything more in the way of thanks for her efforts. Steeling herself for the worst, she walked in to find Dr. Weiss was standing at the window looking out at the lovely spring day. Even more surprising was that upon hearing her entering the room, he quickly turned to see her and actually smiled, albeit ever so slightly.

"Good morning, Miss Holden. Thank you again for pinch-hitting for Mr. Lew last Saturday night."

"Thank you for asking me to join you on stage. It was an evening I will never forget. Heifetz was amazing. And you, Dr. Weiss, performed perfectly."

"Perfection is an ideal…and aspiration, Miss Holden. But thank you," Weiss countered. "By the way, I saw you as I was departing from the lobby that evening. Was that your fiancée or boyfriend with you?"

"No, Dr. Weiss, I'm unattached, though I suspect that gentleman is interested in pursuing something more serious. He's a physician in the Cleveland area and the son of the pastor of the Methodist church where I am the accompanist." As she spoke, she wondered if perhaps she was providing too much information. In order to change the subject, she clumsily inquired about whether his wife was able to travel with him to see the performance.

"No... no, I, too, am unattached. It hasn't always been so, for I was once married when I was your age, but only for a few years. My former wife seemed to enjoy the status of being married to a university professor, but not necessarily the income level. She took up with another man who is somehow able to provide her with the things she wanted in life, and clearly, I wasn't one of those things," Weiss declared in a noticeably bitter tone.

"I'm sorry," Page injected. "I really didn't mean to..."

"Don't apologize, Miss Holden. I brought it up. I should have exercised better judgment. These aren't things to burden you with. It's not important. Now let's get back to your final recital number."

The remaining practice time flew by, and Page was getting very anxious about her final recital. There was more than just completion of her degree program at stake, because her grades put her in the running for graduating with honors. She'd chosen a very difficult piece, and it was going to take all she had in her to perform it well enough to capture the highest grade. However, the one thing that might help her most, she concluded, was that Professor Weiss actually seemed to be more supportive of her now—though no less demanding.

Wednesday night choir practice at the church brought an interesting turn of events. Pastor Robertson walked into the sanctuary about the time things were wrapping up and the singers were making their way into the robe room. He waved Page over to tell her his son had called him and then had asked if she was available to speak to him. The pastor guided Page back to his office where she could see the black phone receiver sitting on the desk. As she went to pick it up, she noticed Pastor Robertson slipping out of the room to allow her some privacy.

"Hello. . . this is Page."

"Wonderful to hear your voice again, Page," responded John cheerfully on the other end. "I was just speaking with my father about coming to Columbus this weekend to take care of some yard work for him. Unfortunately, I've got a late shift in the ER Friday night, so I won't arrive in Columbus until after I've had some time to sleep that off on Saturday. Would you be willing to attend if we hosted you at the parsonage for dinner that evening? I'd really like to see you."

Alarm bells were going off in her head as Page recalled what her mother referred to as "missionary dating"—the practice of going out with a nonbeliever in hopes that he might become a believer. However, she figured with Pastor Robertson there, perhaps it might be all right—not like a real date, that is.

"Certainly, I'd be happy to join you two fine gentlemen for dinner. Tell me what I can bring to add to the affair?"

"No need to bring anything, just a simple dinner. But come good and hungry, because I'll be making my specialty that night."

"Oh, and what might that be?" asked Page as she mentally noted that her own father could barely make toast.

"I make a mean chicken and dumplings, the kind of meal that sticks to your ribs. I look forward to seeing you then. I should be done with all the chores at his place by

five p.m. so let's say six o'clock for dinner. And do you need
a ride over to the house?"

Page indicated that she'd prefer to walk over as daylight
savings time meant plenty of light. She agreed to be there
but insisted on bringing some home-baked cookies, which
John didn't object to one bit.

Chapter 23

Since it was to be a casual affair at the parsonage that Saturday evening, Page wore her white pedal pushers and a red cotton sleeveless shirt. It was pleasant evenings walk over to the house not far from the church, with temperatures in the low seventies. She had baked a few dozen snickerdoodles and wrapped a dozen with plastic cling wrap to carry with her. Though she'd sometimes made cookies for her younger piano students last year, it wasn't something she had much time for while in school. However, she thought she'd be glad to have the extras around the apartment as she entered into finals week preparations.

Arriving just moments before the appointed time, she was greeted at the door by Pastor Robertson, who was quite pleased to see her. As she passed through the entry hallway of the old home, she heard the grandfather clock chime six bells. The pastor brought her into the living room at the back of the house, where she could see a dining table off to one side that was set simply for three. Just as she was about to ask where to place the cookies, John walked out of the nearby kitchen wiping his hands on a dish towel.

"Well, well, dessert has arrived... and cookies too," John said a bit under his breath, though Page was certain his father heard the announcement. While she could feel her face flush with embarrassment, John just winked and gladly accepted the snickerdoodles.

"There, Page, don't mind John," the pastor said in a soothing voice. It was clear he had heard the comment and was trying to make her feel at ease. She quickly forgot the whole thing and moved to be seated in a comfy chair that Pastor Robertson guided her to.

"This must be your favorite chair," said Page in a some-what questioning fashion.

"Well, yes, but I'm perfectly willing to let you sit in it. You are, after all, the guest of honor!"

While the two chatted for a few minutes, John was bring-ing items to the table from the kitchen and pouring lemon-ade for all. Soon he was waving them over to the table to be seated. And with that, Pastor Robertson bowed his head and spoke a prayer of thanks. Page had her eyes closed, but even before the "amen" was uttered, she opened them to see John with his eyes closed and head bowed.

The threesome proceeded to have a wide-ranging dis-cussion about what Page was facing in the way of finishing up her degree, the yard work that John had been doing ear-lier, and what would be the sermon subject for the next day. The chicken and dumpling feast was also a subject for discussion as it was excellent, and Page was certain to say so.

After dinner was consumed, John suggested they take their lemonade glasses out to the back porch to sit on the patio. "I'll be right out with the cookies to join you two," he indicated. But Page was quick to ask if she might help with clearing the table and cleaning up in the kitchen. John wouldn't hear of it and shooed her and his father out toward the back door to the patio.

It was now evening, so most of the patio was shaded, and they could sit on the folding lawn chairs that were there for just these kinds of days. Page and the pastor were making themselves comfortable when John appeared with a plate holding her homemade cookies and offered them to her and his father before setting the plate on a nearby ledge of the small patio half wall.

The three resumed their discussion while admiring all the mowing and planting John had accomplished in the backyard. But within thirty minutes or so, Pastor Robertson excused himself to put the final touches on his sermon. Page thanked him for his hospitality, to which he humbly responded, "John did all the work. I just live here!"

Once John and Page were alone, he pulled his chair a bit closer to hers. A mere two minutes into the conversation, he took her hand. Page looked at their hands together as though she were detached from what she was seeing, as though her hand belonged to someone else. She couldn't help but notice his strong hand, and she wondered how many lives his hands had saved in that emergency room where he worked. As she was thinking it, she found herself asking him, "John, tell me about your shift last night in the ER."

"There is really not much that's pleasant to discuss, Page. In fact, a Friday night in Cleveland can bring lots of difficult emergency cases. Are you sure you want to know?" he asked.

"Yes, I want to know what your life is like."

"Well, last night brought us one domestic abuse victim, a woman in preterm labor, two cases of food poisoning, an asthmatic child, a broken hip, appendicitis, and a heart attack—along with the less serious matters," John reviewed, as though he was reading off a grocery list.

"Did anyone die last night?" asked a very serious Page.

John's voice lowered as he responded with, "Yes, Page, two people died in our ER last night. Please don't ask me to go beyond that. I'd rather not expose you to such things. You're like a delicate flower—a beautiful one at that. It doesn't feel right to talk with you about such things. In fact, let's take a walk. I thought we could walk over to the church so I could hear you play the piece you'll be performing for your final exam. Would you do that for me?"

"I am still a few weeks from having to perform, so I can't promise perfection," Page said haltingly, for in that moment she remembered Professor Weiss telling her that perfection was an ideal. She fell silent for several seconds as she remembered how he played flawlessly and seemingly effortlessly at the concert this month. It was that kind of skill she wanted to own.

As she stared off into the distance deep in thought, John excused himself to get the church key from his father. She wandered back into the house to return the glasses and cookies to the kitchen. John found her there and flashed the key saying, "I can't wait to hear you play. Afterward, I'll walk you home."

The few blocks to the church went quickly as Page filled in the blanks for John about her schedule the next several weeks leading up to graduation in early June. She even broke the news that she could be graduating with honors, but so much of that hinged on her final recital performance.

When the two arrived at the church, John escorted Page to the rear door, where the Pastor typically entered to get to his office. The old church was a bit dark, so he flipped on a few lights as they made their way to the sanctuary. John seemed to be quite comfortable as he found his place in the front pew closest to the piano.

"Take your time, Page... there's no pressure here—it's just me," John assured her.

His words were kind, but for some reason, Page was feeling some pressure to get through the piece, out of the building, and back onto the public sidewalks. She took a deep breath and positioned her hands over the keys and began the difficult étude. She could feel that she was playing too fast leading into the halfway mark of the piece, but by the four minute mark, she seemed to regain control and finished out the piece beautifully.

"Bravo, bravo!" shouted John as he stood up and clapped at the end of the dramatic piece. Page stood up and took a quick bow and then asked John if they could leave now, making some excuse about needing fresh air. He was very accommodating, and they made their way out the back, systematically turning off all the lights as they went. Once John had locked the door, the two were standing in the back parking lot as dusk was starting to take hold. Page inhaled deeply in relief, and it must have shown because John asked her if she was all right. She answered affirmatively, but he didn't seem convinced. When they reached the sidewalk, Page was starting to relax again as they headed toward her apartment via a more circuitous route that took them onto the lovely campus oval.

"Page, that really was well done. It appears to me that you are more than ready for this recital. It seems like a difficult composition. Is the grading anything like Olympic diving or skating where you can get more points for choosing to play a difficult number?"

"Oh, I suppose there is some sense of that in the minds of those who make these determinations, but it's not really a matter of points. I think the closest as it gets to the Olympics is the competition. While my classmates have all been supportive on some level, the truth is, this is a very competitive sport in graduate school," Page responded.

Before departing the campus property, John asked Page to sit with him on a grassy berm as the sun was setting on this warm spring evening. Once seated, it seemed that John wanted to say something but was having a hard time getting it out. It started out slow... but ended like a speeding bullet.

"Page, as you know, I am a single man with a busy life in Cleveland. It is certainly a very solitary life right now. Though I throw myself into my work, there are many times I've wished for companionship—someone with whom I could share my hopes, dreams, and home. Now that you are about to finish your academic program, I wonder if you would consider the possibility of being that companion. What do you say to that idea?" asked John.

Page was stunned silent.

CHAPTER 24

When Page arose the next morning, her head was still spinning from the walk home the night before. In her head, she replayed the conversation over again this morning, especially the part where John told her that he had "hoped to pop the question" while they were in the church last night except that she seemed in such a rush to depart.

She had told John that the whole thing was so sudden that she'd have to think about it. But now she was kicking herself for putting off the inevitable, for she knew in her heart that something—many things—were not right with this picture. As handsome, kind, and successful as John was, Page knew he wasn't the one for her, at least not as things stood at this time.

It was a bit of a relief to know that John would be heading back to Cleveland this morning, even while she was doing her usual routine of accompanying the choir. She was also eager to depart for Hudson right after church for an early Memorial Day celebration with her family. She'd only have about twenty-four hours before having to turn right around to take her finals this week. Right now she just wanted to confide in her mother.

The service went well, and there was no hint from Pastor Robertson that he had any idea what his son had said to her. Immediately after the service, she jumped in her car, which she had driven to church for the purpose of making a quick getaway afterward. All the way to Hudson, she returned to the conversation with John the night before. She found herself in one moment feeling flattered that someone would want to marry her, then in another moment, she would wonder what he saw in her, and in yet another moment, she'd panic that if she said no to his request she'd end up an old spinster. She even tried not to think about it at all, but her mind would wander back to the fact that such a thing was worth thinking about because of the gravity and impact of such a decision.

Pulling into the driveway just after noon, Page realized there was a gnawing in her stomach from having had nothing but coffee for breakfast. She pulled her overnight bag and purse from the passenger's seat and flung open the car door only to find Maggie lumbering toward her across the lawn. Knowing Maggie couldn't get out of the house by herself, Page looked toward the house to see her father standing at the screen door and holding it open for her.

"Oh, Daddy, it's great to be home!" shouted Page.

In her father's usual deep-chested loving tones he simply said, "It's great to have you home, baby."

The moment she stepped into the house Page was overwhelmed by the feelings of contentment she felt there. Her dad gave her a big hug and pointed to the kitchen indicating where she could find her mom, though it wasn't hard to tell Ellen Holden was cooking due to the yummy smells that permeated the house. Ducking into the kitchen, Page found her mother pulling the husks off of fresh corn on the cob.

"What's this? Something different today?" she inquired.

Her mother replied with a wink saying, "Hi, sweetie. I decided to have our Memorial Day picnic today since you won't be here for the holiday. Are you ready for a barbeque?"

"Wow, Mom, that sounds and smells wonderful!"

The meal of barbequed pulled pork sandwiches, corn on the cob, coleslaw, and iced tea was a big hit. Page sat in amazement watching her brother down two helpings of everything, including the peach pie for dessert. Every time someone asked her how things were going she talked about school and avoided any discussion about John. She wanted to speak to her mother alone about that one, because she felt only another woman would understand—and Mom seemed to always understand.

Thankfully, much of the dinner conversation was taken up with Jeff's tales from his senior year. He'd been the captain of the track team, had lettered in track, and had even worked up the nerve to ask one of the pretty drill team girls to the prom. The only thing that struck a difficult note for the entire family was when the now 18-year-old brought up the fact that he'd fulfilled his required duty of registering for the draft and was wondering what might happen with that now that he was graduating.

After lunch, her father and brother announced that they were going to get the bikes out of the barn, pump up the tires, and go for a ride. It was a perfect day for a bike ride, and if Page hadn't already planned to discuss her situation with her mother, she would have arm wrestled with her kid brother for that first ride. The guys left the house, and Page immediately went into the kitchen to help her mother clean up.

"Mom, there's something I need to talk to you about," said Page as she picked up a dish in shaky hands.

"Sure thing. What's up, Page?" Her mother watched her, gently taking the dish out of her hands.

Page averted her eyes. "Well, last night that doctor I told you about proposed to me... well, at least that was how I took it."

"How else could one take such a thing, Page?" Her mother put the dish down and led Page to a seat at the kitchen table. "What do you mean? Either he did or he didn't. That's usually how it works."

"Yes, well, he said he was looking for companionship, and I took that to mean marriage. What else could that mean anyway?"

Mrs. Holden sighed. "These days, it's a bit harder to know what they mean when they say that. But, no matter— I thought you had crossed this guy off the list because he doesn't share your values and faith. You haven't led him on, have you, Page?"

"No... or at least I don't think I have." Page turned to her mother and tried to explain the set of circumstances that led to this surprising request.

After all was out in the open, her mother quietly and methodically responded.

"So let me understand this... and you listen very carefully to what I'm reflecting back to you, Page. This young man never told you he loved you. Then he proposed 'companionship'—not marriage. He laid out his thinking from the perspective of his own loneliness. Then he indicated he wanted to ask you this question in the church because he 'knows how important that is to *you.*' Am I getting all this right?"

Page was staring at the table as her mother recounted the whole thing correctly. She nodded her head up and down and then tears began to stream down her cheeks. Her mother set down the dish towel in her hand and opened her arms wide as Page broke down in them. As she wept on her mother's shoulder, Mrs. Holden didn't say a word. There was nothing more to say, and Page knew it. She knew it before she even arrived home, but somehow her mother had a way of bringing matters into clear focus.

The two women remained at the table while Page pulled herself together. But through her sniffles, Page asked, "Oh, Mom, what if no one ever wants to marry me?"

"Page, dear, someone will undoubtedly ask. You are a beautiful and gifted young woman, and life has only just begun for you. This doctor knows a good thing when he sees it, but he's asking for all the wrong things for all the wrong reasons. You deserve much more than that. You deserve the fullness of life that God has always intended for you. Don't panic... after all, God isn't panicked. He knows the plans he has for you."

With a good night's sleep and her mother's wisdom ringing in her ears, Page set off the next afternoon for her last days of school. With the final recital ahead of her on Friday, followed by graduation ceremonies the week after that, Page was refocused and determined to finish strong. Hugging her father, brother, and mother before departing, she thanked them for everything. She told them how much she was looking forward to their coming down to Columbus for her graduation on Friday, June 8, when they would also celebrate her twenty-fourth birthday, as well as Jeff's high school graduation. As she walked out the door, her father followed her. Handing her a twenty dollar bill this time, he hinted that she might want to get a dress or have her hair done for graduation. "You know, whatever it is you ladies do for special occasions," he said with a wink.

CHAPTER 25

The first of June had arrived, and Page was a bundle of nerves as she stood behind the heavy, blue curtains of the filled-to-capacity recital hall. She had drawn the last number of all the graduate students and felt the weight of it, knowing that her performance would be left standing in the minds of attendees. Doubts crept in, but she'd dashed them against the rocks of confidence as she envisioned herself giving her best performance of all time. Like an athlete, she'd done all her preparation and was ready for action.

Page heard her student number called, for that was all the competitors were now—just a number. She stepped out from behind the drapes and into the light and stifling silence of the crowd. It wasn't a graduation day outfit that she had spent her money on but a beautiful, black, fitted-bodice, full-length V-neck dress with a deep shawl drape in the back for this occasion. The saleswoman who talked her into the pricey number told her she looked like Audrey Hepburn in the stunning dress. Page smiled inside as she walked toward the padded bench seat, remembering when her father had mentioned her resemblance to the famous actress when he saw her senior picture in her high school yearbook. Though she knew her father was working today, it still made her wish he could see her now.

As she sat down and set her feet, Page took a deep breath before lifting her hands to the keyboard. When ready she began the heavy lifting of the Transcendental étude no. 10 in F Minor by Franz Liszt. She entered the piece with all its beauty and continued to bring out the passion of its deep refrain. Page had first heard the thrilling étude played by the brilliant Adele Marcus via a recording played on the radio a few years earlier. She loved it from start to finish over the nearly five minutes it took to play. She recalled that when she had announced to Professor Weiss that this was to be her final recital selection, he initially tried to talk her out of it due to the level of difficulty. However, when he heard her play it in raw form without the discipline he would bring to bear upon her playing, he conceded that he thought it had potential. He had issues with her hands moving above the fallboard and other excess movement during the early days of practice, but she had taken every bit of his advice to achieve what he referred to as "expression made to look easy."

Today Page would complete her recital number with skill and meaning. From the beginning of the strenuous piece to the point at which she lifted her hands from the piano and began to stand, she was almost unaware of the audience due to her total immersion in the music. She didn't even care that a piece of her bangs that she thought she had sprayed into place had fallen over her left eye again.

But as she rose from the bench, it was as though her senses returned her to reality—a moment where there was generous clapping and several attendees were standing. Page looked out at her fellow students in amazement because she knew they'd all been instructed this time not to make any display before or after any of the students played. Trying not to burst with tears of joy, she noticed that even some of her instructors were standing. As she searched the crowd to gauge the response from Professor Weiss, she found his usual front-row seat was empty. Had he missed the whole thing? Page hurried off the stage and out toward the curtain just as the department chairman was thanking all the students and attendees for their hard work over the school year.

Pulling back the drape, she found herself moving briskly to the solace of her old piano practice room where she thought she might be able to close the door, catch her breath, and just relax for a while. As she walked swiftly but quietly into the room, it took a second or two before she noticed Professor Weiss leaning toward the window with both hands on the sill as he stared at the hedges on the other side of the glass. He seemed so deep in thought that she considered backing up slowly to exit the space, but he dropped his hands from the sill and turned toward her too quickly. Her heart was pounding as she didn't want to know if he had skipped her performance. And if he hadn't, she didn't want to hear any criticism after being on cloud nine from what she considered to be her best performance ever. There she stood, in the middle of the room as if frozen, when he spoke a simple, "Miss Holden?"

"I'm sorry for interrupting, Professor. I was just seeking out a quiet space..." was all she could muster up.

"Don't apologize, Miss Holden. You may have your quiet space, but only after I tell you that you performed splendidly today. I'm not allowed to weigh into your final recital grade because of the potential for bias as your coach, but I'm certain that your overall grades, combined with exceptional work in the recital, will net you an excellent cumulative grade point average," the professor stated calmly.

"Thank you, Professor Weiss. I hope my grades will allow me to graduate with honors. But after hearing Jun Lew deliver a perfect recital with that Rachmaninoff prelude, I'm certain he'll graduate summa cum laude," responded Page.

"I suspect you may be correct, Miss Holden, though you have finished well, and there's still the possibility of cum laude honors. Now, I'll leave you to your thoughts," the professor said as he made his way past her and exited the small room.

Page collapsed on the chair near the music stand—a chair she'd never sat in before today... his chair. She thought she should be gathering with her fellow students to congratulate them but decided she'd wait until tonight's ice cream social over at the student union where all the graduate music majors would be gathering. Certainly she wanted to speak with Jun, Alison, Peggy, and Jean—her hometown friend and high school classmate who was a voice major. She could feel exhaustion overtaking her. Alone with her thoughts, Page replayed the recital and the whole academic year in her head, all the while wondering what the Lord had in store for her after all this.

CHAPTER 26

The weekend was a welcome relief to Page. The pressure was off, and even Vivian Backlund had agreed to give her the Sunday off since the choir wasn't going to be singing due to a visiting soloist performing. As Page rolled out of bed at nearly ten a.m. on Saturday, she reflected on what a luxury it was to sleep in so late. She needed it because she had stayed pretty late at the party over at the student union. She received lots of congratulations from her classmates, including Jun Lew, who kept reminding her that the composition she chose was so much more difficult than his. Jun wasn't one to hand out many compliments, but he had been very gracious toward her.

Page had broken away from her piano compatriots long enough to spend a good two hours with Jean and her husband Tom. Jean and Page had grown up together, but while Page went to Ohio Wesleyan for her undergraduate years, Jean had entered Ohio State for her music degree. Jean had met T. Elliot Brown in their senior year when they were "set up" by a mutual friend to attend a traditional annual event sponsored by the Epsilon Psi Epsilon optometry fraternity where Tom was chapter president. The two were inseparable after their first encounter, ended up marrying last spring, and were now living in married student housing on campus while they continued their studies.

Page had a blast catching up with Jean and getting to know her husband. She had spent her youth hearing Jean's beautiful voice in Girl Scouts, summer church camp, and the high school choir. The two had once performed together at a junior class banquet where Page accompanied Jean, who sang a popular Broadway tune from *My Fair Lady*. And, earlier in the day, Jean had heard from another friend about her teaching contract decision. It seemed the friend was contemplating backing out, leaving an opening for a high school music teacher. Page pronounced that she would drop off her resume with the school principal on Monday morning.

Page couldn't help but notice how happy Tom and Jean seemed to be together. And while she was happy for them, it reminded her that she still owed Dr. Robertson quite literally a "Dear John" letter. This morning she woke up to that chore—one that she'd need to take care of right away.

After cleaning up the apartment, doing some laundry, getting some groceries at the store, it was the afternoon when Page sat down to write the note.

> Dear John,
>
> I've given your "proposal" much thought over the course of this busy week at school. I want to preface my comments by saying how much I have appreciated our friendship and our time together. Having said that, I hope you will understand when I say that I don't believe we are a well-suited couple. As much fun as we've had,

and as kind as you are, there remains a gap between us that cannot be bridged as long as we don't share the same faith. I cannot spend the rest of my life with someone who simply tolerates something that is central to my being—and that's the One who was, and is, and is to come—Jesus Christ.

Despite this, I am more than willing to maintain a cordial friendship and will continue to pray for you.

I trust all is going well for you in your job at the hospital. I have completed my final recital and am now just awaiting my final grades before graduation next weekend. My family members are driving down for the big day. I can hardly believe how quickly the year has gone by. Not sure of my future at this point, but I know who holds the future so I am in good hands.

All the best,

Page

Placing the folded note into an envelope, Page addressed the letter to John's Cleveland address, licked the stamp, and walked the letter out to the corner mailbox where she just caught the mailman doing his late Saturday run. Taking the envelope from her, he wished her a pleasant evening—which was exactly what she had at home... alone.

CHAPTER 27

Grades were to be available at the School of Music by Tuesday afternoon, so Page took a leisurely stroll across campus to see the verdict. As she was walking past her old practice room, she couldn't help but notice Professor Weiss coming down the hallway toward her. He seemed so much more at ease now that school was over, or perhaps it was his casual summer attire that made him look more relaxed. When he looked up from his papers in hand to see her, he stopped and put out his hand to shake hers. She reciprocated but promptly inquired, "What's this for?"

"Oh, you haven't seen the bulletin board yet? Well, young lady, you received a perfect grade on your final recital and will be graduating magna cum laude."

Page was still shaking his hand while taking in the wonderful news but then couldn't resist throwing her arms around his neck in sheer joy. "Oh, Professor Weiss, I couldn't have done it without you! I just wish you hadn't been so hard on me all year," she blurted out before even realizing how it sounded.

The professor stepped back and gave her a stern look, making Page think she'd truly offended him. But within seconds, it was clear he couldn't hold back a smile as he said, "Miss Holden, I am only hard on my best students—the ones who show the greatest potential. Now, step into the practice room and tell me about your plans going forward."

Page followed him to the room where she sat on the bench while he took his usual folding chair, though he turned it backward before sitting down. She began to tell the professor that she wasn't sure if she should pursue a doctorate or teach music at the secondary level. The professor responded rapidly with, "Page... do you mind if I call you Page? Well, in any event, I would encourage you not to waste time with such things. I understand that the Columbus Symphony Orchestra is seeking a regular pianist. I know the board chairwoman from having assisted them in the search for a conductor a few years back. I will speak with her on your behalf—assuming you're interested, of course. And if they engage you, I am willing to continue private lessons if you are interested."

"Oh my, Professor, you would be willing to recommend me for such a position? Why, I hardly know what to say. And private tutoring with you—well, I need to pray about all this."

"Pray? Oh yes, you're the praying type. I should have such faith, so who am I to talk?" the professor said with a bit of a chuckle.

"Oh, but you can!" said Page with even greater excitement.

"Were I to pray to your Jesus, I'm afraid my dear widowed Jewish mother would disown me—and then she'd hunt me down and kill me!" the professor responded with a grin. "Now give me your phone number so I can arrange for you to meet with the symphony as soon as possible. I don't know where they are in their process of trying to fill this position, but I want to make sure they consider you."

As Page called out her phone number, the professor wrote it on the palm of his hand with his pen and then asked her to stay in the room while he went to his office to see if he could reach the chairwoman by phone. In the few minutes that Page waited patiently on the bench, her thoughts and heart soared at the idea of landing such an incredible job after graduation. She whispered a prayer, "Lord, if it be your will."

Before long the professor returned to the room with news that she had an audition late tomorrow afternoon with the symphony conductor. He handed her a piece of paper containing the conductor's name as well as that of the board chairwoman, who she was to speak with on the Monday after graduation. He was rubbing her phone number off his hand while informing her that she was to meet him at the entrance of a tearoom inside a local department store downtown where he would introduce her to the wealthy woman. Once again, Page wanted to throw her arms around Professor Weiss, but she resisted the urge, believing that she'd already been inappropriate when she did so earlier in the hallway. Instead she thanked him profusely and told him she'd see him at the tearoom promptly at eleven-thirty a.m. on the following Monday.

CHAPTER 28

Graduation day had finally arrived, and what a spectacular day it was—a bit hazy in the morning, but that gave way to a gorgeous blue sky dotted with the occasional puffy cloud passing through. The ceremony would be held at the Ohio Stadium on this Friday morning. And despite it being a banking day, Mr. Holden had taken the day off to bring Mrs. Holden and Jeff down to Columbus for the big event. Page always appreciated that her little family was always there for each other, in big and small ways.

As Page stood in line with the graduate students from the School of Music, she was doing a last minute fix of her hood, mortar board, and tassels. She'd be second in line behind Jun Lew, who would be returning to China for further studies after attaining summa cum laude. The whole thing was terribly exciting as the guides waved them all through to take their correct spot in the correct seats once they entered the stadium. Once seated, the graduates would observe all the pomp of their academic leaders, hear from President Fawcett, and then listen to the graduation speech by the Air Force Chief of Staff from the Department of Defense.

But before all the events of the morning began, the students took a few minutes to locate their families in the stands and wave to them. Page found the Holden gang exactly where they said they'd be. In fact, as she spotted her father, he held up a handmade cardboard sign with the words "That's My Girl" in bright red paint.

The graduation speaker talked to the graduates briefly while driving home his main point that their diploma wasn't just a "work permit" but a ticket to a great future in this nation of opportunity. It was both inspiring and a bit overwhelming. Page enjoyed the speech, but, as was so often the case, graduation speakers rarely seemed to address those in the arts. Instead, these space-age days seemed ripe for those in the sciences, engineering, and technology. Nevertheless, she was determined to use the gifts that God had given her and not hide them or waste them.

As the procession of students finally arrived after all the speeches, the graduate students went first and took far less time than the many undergraduates. The graduate students filed past the riser where the faculty was sitting. Page spotted Dr. Weiss sitting in his very impressive academic regalia. He seemed to follow her with his eyes. Page went through the line, shook the dean's hand, and received her diploma. She was now officially a master of piano.

After the family was reunited, they headed over to a local restaurant on the outskirts of town for a big feast to celebrate Page's new degree, Jeff's high school diploma, and her twenty-fourth birthday. Her mother had made reservations, and everyone was plenty hungry after the ceremony. The food was simple but tasty, and Page loved the yeast rolls so much that she was tempted to make a meal of them.

For her birthday, Page was given a new handbag to replace the one she'd been carrying all school year that was now looking pretty shabby. Her brother had gone the distance by buying Page a new wallet to go inside. And just to round things out, her father had put a crisp hundred-dollar bill inside the wallet. One hundred dollars was a tidy sum for a graduation gift, and Page was already thinking about how she might spend some of the money while also putting some away in her small savings account. There were also graduation gifts and a fifty-dollar bill presented to Jeff for his graduation, though Page couldn't help but notice that Jeff seemed a bit subdued throughout the dinner. She hoped her major life event wasn't overshadowing his and did her best to make a big fuss over him.

As the fun and hugs went all around the table, Page finally found the right opening to tell her family that she had what she felt was a successful audition just forty-eight hours earlier with the Columbus Symphony conductor, and she would be meeting the board chair next Monday for an interview. Her mother was almost ready to burst with excitement, and her father was button-busting proud of his daughter. Even her less-than-expressive brother was impressed and happy for her. As they talked about how the interview had come about, the family was taken aback by the fact that "Not-so-Nice Weiss" had been the one to recommend her for the position. Page went on to tell them about how much the professor's approach had actually spurred her on to a higher skill level, and now that classes were over, he'd softened his edges quite a bit. She even mentioned that he had offered to privately coach her if she landed the job, though she didn't bring up any particulars about that. After all, first she had to get the job—and she had no idea what her competition might be.

When two p.m. rolled around and everyone had eaten their fill, Page was overwhelmed by the generosity of her family. To think she was given so many nice gifts, not to mention eating out at a restaurant, which was something her family only did four or five times a year. She was feeling pretty special and gave everyone a hug as they dropped her off back at her apartment. Her father reminded her to write or call home the minute she had an update on her job possibilities at the symphony or the school district. Her mother reminded her that if one of these jobs didn't work out, then the Lord must have something else in mind for her. Though Page could rest in that thought, she was already daydreaming about getting the symphony job. But something else remained with her as she watched her family drive away that late afternoon... the unease she sensed from her little brother.

CHAPTER 29

On Monday morning, Page was trying to figure out what to wear to this important interview. With blouses and skirts strewn around the apartment, she was starting to panic. Would this woman like her? What did the conductor tell her about her audition results? What had the professor told the chairwoman of the symphony board?

In the end, she settled not on a blouse and skirt but on one of her few dresses. It was a perfectly fitted mint-green collarless shirt dress with a self-belt. Adding a double-stranded pearl necklace seemed to class it up a bit, even if they were fakes. Page checked her outfit in the bathroom mirror, but since she had no full-length mirror, it just made her more frustrated that she couldn't see the whole look. As she leaned over to put on her white heels, the pearls leaned with her. Seeing them out of the corner of her eye, she couldn't help but wonder if the interviewer would consider her a fraud too.

None of this self-talk was doing her any good... and she knew it. Stopping to catch her breath before putting the final touches on her hair and makeup, Page slowly walked over to her small dining table and sat down. Folding her hands in front of her, she looked upward and began to pray.

"Lord, I'm a nervous wreck over this interview. I suppose I don't need to tell you that—you know me inside and out. But I am pleading with you to calm my heart and allow me to lean on you in this entire matter. Because you know me, you know my heart's desire is to land this position with the symphony. However, not my will, but yours be done. Amen."

With minutes to spare, Page walked down the department store's main aisle toward the open glass doors of the tearoom entrance. Her mind was set at ease to see Professor Weiss standing at the entrance with a matronly looking woman of short stature. As the professor spotted Page, he reached out to shake her hand in serious formality. He said her name and proceeded to introduce the women to each other.

Soon the three were escorted into the tearoom to a table for two, and Page was certain there must be some mistake. Before she uttered a word, the professor was assisting the dowager with her dining chair. He then moved toward the second chair and pulled it out for Page. She began to sit down while looking at him with a fear that he might not stay to support her.

"Page, I will leave you two to discuss the position at the symphony. I'm not one who frequents ladies tearooms, but I did want to make sure the connection was made. Enjoy your lunch, ladies," the professor stated with aplomb as he began to withdraw.

Shaken but trying to remain focused, Page said her gracious goodbyes to the professor and quickly turned her attention to the loyal patron of the symphony. As the conversation moved from niceties, to eating, to discussions of their respective backgrounds, Page found herself relaxing and enjoying the fascinating community leader. In fact, the more they talked, the more they found themselves laughing. Before long, an entire hour had passed, and the two were finishing up their citrus tea and swan-shaped cream puff desserts. Page couldn't help but think that even if she didn't get the job, she was certainly having a wonderful time seeing how the other half lived.

As the bill was paid by the gracious arts patron and the two were wrapping things up, Page decided to go out on a limb and ask when the symphony might be making a decision about their pianist for this season. No sooner had she gotten her question out than the woman stood up as if to depart, so Page quickly stood as well. The lovely lady pulled a beautiful embroidered handkerchief from her purse and then crossed her arms with that same purse in the crook of her left arm. She leaned toward Page and in a whispered tone said, "Miss Holden, I would have you consider the position with a salary of $8,000 for the forty weeks of service, starting in mid-September. Does that seem reasonable to you?"

Page thought she might have not heard the women correctly, so she repeated the terms before immediately following that with, "Absolutely! I accept!"

CHAPTER 30

While making her way back to the apartment that afternoon, Page felt she was floating rather than driving. Her head was swimming with thoughts about the job and about getting to meet with the conductor of the symphony again later this week. The brilliant day was a reflection of her sunny mood and excitement about her future.

No sooner had she inserted her key in the locked apartment door than she realized that she must thank Professor Weiss this very afternoon. Even though she wasn't sure he'd be at the music building, she decided to put on more comfortable clothes and walking shoes to make her way there to thank him in person.

Page walked briskly across campus and into the music building assuming she'd try to locate the professor in his office, but on her way, she passed by the large recital hall and heard music coming from inside. If it was the professor, she was determined to make an obvious entry and not hang back in the wings as she had before. As she entered in, Page found him sitting on the piano bench making beautiful music, though she was not familiar with the piece he was playing. She stood frozen in place in the aisle as he played. So much for her determination to let her presence be known, she thought. While her mind was momentarily searching for a reason why she had stopped, an alarming realization came crashing in on her as she watched him play. He enchanted her.

Playing and holding the final chords, Professor Weiss then slowly took his strong hands from the piano and crossed his arms over his chest as if sitting in judgment of his own work. Page cleared her throat to announce herself, and he quickly turned to see her walking down the aisle toward the stage. As she did, he waved her over, shifted his body to the left on the bench seat, and patted the remaining open space as an invitation for her to sit down next to him there. Page was confused by his friendly gesture but made her way to the bench while complimenting him on his playing.

"Ah, that was a lesser known number that I recently heard a recording of—played by the Hungarian pianist, Cziffra. I consider him to be one of the finest pianists of all time," responded the professor.

Immediately and with great excitement, Page announced that she'd been offered the job at the symphony. As she slowly sat down next to the professor, her shoulder brushed against his, and she even caught the faint scent of his aftershave.

"I know. Congratulations, Page, you are going to thrive in that organization," he responded in an affirming and calm voice. Page was about to launch into her gratitude for the job recommendation when he reached for the gold cross that hung on her necklace. Holding it in the palm of his hand while staring at it and then letting it gently fall back upon her chest, he said, "I've been reading about your Jesus lately—in the so-called 'New Testament.'"

"Oh, good," Page said, while suddenly feeling self-conscious about her response...and being this close to her professor. "You can hardly reject what you don't know, so I'm glad to hear you are reading the New Testament," she continued.

Awkward silence ensued as she looked over at his casual white oxford shirt that was open at the neck where she saw the gold chain he wore underneath. In a daring move, she reached for the chain and slowly pulled it out from his shirt. He didn't stop her as her eyes gazed upon the beautiful encircled gold Star of David.

"You know, I'd be glad to try to answer any questions you might have about what you're reading—and about the one King David called 'The Son,'" she said softly as she continued holding the weighty star in her hand.

This close, they could almost feel each other's breath. He responded by turning toward her saying, "I'll be sure to ask the Bible teacher my questions, if she'll just stop talking long enough for me to kiss her." With that, his full lips were hovering over hers until neither one could resist any longer. Page melted away at his warm kiss, which seemed to last a while before she came to her senses. Pulling away, she exclaimed, "Oh, dear, we can't be doing this—you're my teacher!"

A beautiful smile came over his handsome face as he looked at her with his soft brown eyes. Putting his hand on her shoulder, he responded, "Page, we are no longer in a student-faculty status. I am no longer your teacher, unless of course you want to take me up on those lessons I offered on a private basis. Speaking of private, may I take you to dinner this weekend?"

Page let out a breath as she'd been holding it while he spoke. "Yes, though it's against my better judgment and my mother's advice," she heard herself say.

He began to stand and offered his hand to assist her to stand. Smiling all the while, he said "Well, then I guess we'll just have to agree not to tell our mothers about this."

CHAPTER 31

Page had several seemingly long days to wonder if she should even be going on this date with her former professor. However, she'd also had those days to daydream about him—and that's what worried her. She would even try to muster up her former anger at him for how mean he was to her during the school year, but it was as though those days were now pale and fuzzy in her recollection. By the time Saturday arrived, she'd found herself completely unable to put him out of her mind.

In preparation for the date, Page had to come to terms with her cash on hand. Though it was tempting to dip into the hundred-dollar gift from her parents, she resisted, knowing it would be months before she started her new job. Page concluded that she could either have her hair done or get a new dress for the occasion, but certainly not both. Since she'd put off having her hair done for far too long, it meant an early morning trip to the salon and an afternoon of trying to figure out how she could accessorize something from her existing wardrobe to make it look a bit different. After all, the professor had seen her in everything she owned, many times over. Oh, how she wished she could be standing in that dressing room back in Severance Hall with access to so many beautiful things to wear.

Page also took the time to give herself a manicure and paint her nails with a clear gloss polish. That was something she rarely got to do as she'd grown up being admonished by her piano teachers about never wearing rings, bracelets, or nail polish to lessons or recitals.

In addition to her long black skirt for performances, she also had a short black flared skirt. Coupling the latter with her white shell, she decided to drape a black and white paisley print scarf around the top of the shell and pulled it over to one side to give the outfit a bit of an asymmetrical look. With her white heels and her nylon stockings, the only thing she wished for was a pair of fancy clip-on earrings, but the string of fake pearls was all that Page had in the way of jewelry, besides her cross.

Laying the entire outfit out on her couch, she had one last thought. Perhaps she'd call Jean; certainly she might have some earrings, a bracelet, or something Page could borrow for the dinner date. No sooner had Page picked up the phone to dial up her friend than she promptly hung up over the realization that she'd have to tell Jean who she was going out with tonight. Since the idea of going out with her professor still seemed a bit scandalous to Page, she thought better about borrowing any jewelry.

To preserve her hairdo, Page put her hair in a towel wrap before getting into the shower about an hour before the professor was to pick her up. After getting dressed, she spent the majority of her time digging around in her small makeup bag to come up with an evening look. Though Page wanted to look sophisticated and glamorous tonight, it was a lot to ask of a bit of loose powder, some rouge, old mascara, and a worn-down tube of Tangee natural lipstick.

At exactly six o'clock p.m., there was a knock on her apartment door. Picking up her small white clutch, which contained nothing more than two dimes, her apartment key, and her lipstick, Page opened the door. There on the doormat were six velvety long-stem red roses lying in a white box...but no professor. The bewildered Page stepped out and bent down to pick up the beautiful flowers, and as she began to stand erect, she saw the professor coming out from the late afternoon shadows. Walking toward her in a dark gray suit with a diagonally striped tie of gray, white, and black, he said, "I hope you like roses."

"Of course. I do. Thank you very much."

"Do you need a moment to put them in water before we depart?"

"Why, yes...yes, I do."

"I'll wait right here then. It's a wonderful evening out here," the professor noted.

Page felt bad about leaving him on the doorstep, so she left the door open while she disappeared into the kitchenette to find a tall pitcher. She filled the container with water and put the roses in the water. They casually fell to the rounded sides of the pitcher as she brought the arrangement over to her dining table for two and set them there. The professor looked up, twirled his keychain around his index finger, and winked at her in approval.

As Page reached for her clutch to twist the clasp and pull out the key, the professor stood back as she locked her door. Then he stuck out his elbow for her to accept as he walked her to his car. As they approached his newer black convertible Triumph with camel leather interior, Page panicked inside. All she could think was that the painstaking efforts to preserve her hairdo were a waste. But as the professor was swinging open the small car door for her, he casually mentioned that the scarf around her neck might come in handy in a convertible. Page remarked, "That's why you have a doctorate—you're smart like that." She tugged at the scarf on her shoulder and pulled it off to shape it into a triangle. Placing it over her hair and tying the ends under her chin, she turned to him and smiled. The professor just chortled and said, "Yes, that's it—I knew there was a reason my parents sank so much into my education!"

As the two zipped off down the road, it was Page who spoke first by reaching forward and patting the console saying, "Nice car, Professor."

Never taking his eyes off the road, he responded, "First of all, thank you. It's my pride and joy—my one indulgence. Second, please call me Gavi."

"Gavriel is a beautiful name, almost too wonderful to shorten to Gavi," remarked Page. "However, if you insist. It's going to take some getting used to not to refer to you as Professor Weiss though."

"I like your name too. Page... spelled just like a page in a book. I like books, especially the classics. And you?" he inquired.

"Oh yes, I do like books, but my parents couldn't have known that when they chose to deviate from the traditional spelling of the name," she speculated out loud.

"Well, I hope you also like food. I'm taking you to the Crystal Room over at Hotel Fort Hayes. Are you familiar with it?" he asked.

"I'm famished, though I've never been there. I've only heard about it, because that's not a place that a poor, struggling student can eat, Prof... I mean, Gavi!" Page responded with a nervous laugh.

As they turned onto the road where the hotel stood several stories, Gavi found a parking space along the street.

He explained that he'd need to put the top up as they would be leaving after dark. After parking the car and helping her out onto the sidewalk, he began the task of securing the car and locking the trunk while Page removed her scarf, tied it back around her neck, and fluffed her hair a bit.

The hotel interior was quite elegant, though clearly it dated back several decades. Page was taken by the pretty wallpaper and artwork on the walls. It seemed like such a stately place, and even more so when they entered the Crystal Room with its drapery, paintings, and white linen-covered tables. It was all so elegant that Page definitely felt underdressed. However, she felt less self-conscious when they were seated on the side of the room at a table for two and Gavi casually commented that she "classed up the place."

As the meal progressed from salad to entrée to dessert, the two talked mostly about music and the school year that had just passed. For Page, it was a chance to try to rethink the professor that she had struggled to please for those many months, and for Gavi, it was a chance to open up to her such that she might come to know him as someone other than her instructor. One thing was quite certain between them... there was chemistry. This was never more evident than when Page brought up his offer of private piano lessons. She knew she'd need ongoing performance training in her new job, but she expressed concern about being alone in his home—or even in her apartment.

"Are you afraid to be alone with me?" he asked.

"It's more than just appearances, Gavi."

When he pressed her for what "more than" meant, she could feel the flush of red on her cheeks as she confessed that she was afraid for her heart too. With that, he reached over with his hand to cover her hand that was resting on the table and told her that he'd work something out so that they could practice in a more neutral place—perhaps even at the auditorium where the symphony performed. As she looked down at his hand on hers, all she could think about was how many times she'd looked at those hands play such beautiful music. Now she hoped he'd never take his hand off hers.

As he noticed she was blushing, he did remove his hand and changed the subject. "I've been reading the book of John. Do you know it?" he asked.

"Know it—why, it's my favorite book in the Bible. In fact, the pastor of the Methodist church where I accompany the choir is going to be leading a summer Bible study on that very book. Would you like to tag along with me on Tuesday evenings in July and August?" she inquired.

Gavi ran his fingers straight back through his brown hair and exhaled nervously.

"I've never stepped foot inside a church, not even to play the piano at an event. Look, I have to go out-of-town tomorrow and don't return until late on Friday. It's early June now. Give me some time to warm up to that idea, okay? Let's talk about it when I get back. However, I must say that I'm thrilled that you're willing to see me again."

A peace came over Page about the whole matter of the Bible study class, despite the fact that Gavi seemed anxious about the idea. This time it was her turn to assure him. Reaching over to pat his hand as he picked up the tab, she said, "Thank you for a lovely dinner. We'll talk when you're ready, and I do want to see you again."

The dinner seemed to fly by, and before long, Gavi had Page back on her apartment doorstep. In the glow of the amber porch light hanging next to her front door, they lingered, not wanting to separate. They were just starting to get to know each other on very different terms. However, the professor didn't hesitate to say goodnight with another one of those dreamy melt-away kisses of his.

As Page locked herself in her apartment for the night, all she could think about was how that kiss was the *real* dessert to top off their dinner date. Then in a flash, a terrible thought entered her mind. The professor didn't have her phone number. She'd seen him rub it off of his hand when she provided it for the symphony lady. Oh dear... what if he never called on her again?

CHAPTER 32

Page initiated the week with a phone call to her parents, and it was her father who picked up on the other end.

"Daddy, I got the symphony job! Be sure to let Mom know. I'll be starting in September though, so it could be another lean financial summer. However, I'll stay on at the church and maybe have some piano students. I can't thank you enough for the graduation money; it will help me get by."

"So proud of my girl! And now you're all grown up and a concert pianist—just as you dreamed of being for so many years. But hey, we didn't want you to have to spend your gift money on rent. I'm going to send you a check for July and August rent so you can get by until that first payday. I'll throw in a little extra for gas because I know we're going to want to see you as much as possible this summer."

"Thanks, Dad. You and Mom are so good to me, but I can't wait to be able to have a real salary so that I won't have to be relying on you so much. How's Mom?"

"Well, Page, she's just okay. She's standing right here in the kitchen with me, so I'm going to put her on the phone now. Love you, baby," Mr. Holden signed off.

"Page, first, let me say congratulations! Sounds like you got the job of your dreams. I'm very happy for you. You've worked very hard for this. Now Dad has left the room, and I need to pass along some information that's hit us pretty hard. This morning Jeff informed us that he'd received a reminder of his 1-A draft status in the mail last week. Apparently, he felt it was inevitable that he'd be drafted, so he went ahead and enlisted in the Army and must report to boot camp in July."

Page was gulping hard to swallow the lump rising in her throat.

"Mom, I am proud of Jeff for so many reasons, but I'm so scared for him. Did he tell you and Dad before he did this?"

"Nope... just up and enlisted. We're scared too, Page— but Jeff's an adult, and we're standing in support of his decision to serve. I just wanted you to know... and to pray. He's not home right now, but you might want to give Jeff a call soon. Feel free to call collect if you need to, sweetie."

"Of course I'll talk to him, but it will be pretty hard to keep from crying. In fact, I think I need a good cry after I get off the phone with you, Mom. Please hug Dad for me. I love you all."

"I know, Page—we love you, and I'm doing my own share of crying when Jeff isn't around to see it. Keep in touch, dear."

In between tears and fret over the news, Page felt like the only thing she'd truly accomplished the whole week was her first meeting with the symphony conductor since she had accepted the job. After their lengthy chat, he told her that he was more than delighted that she'd be joining the group. He then loaded her up with sheet music from the many things they'd be tackling in the coming season, which included Beethoven's Piano Concerto no. 4. And that work was something she felt certain she'd need coaching on.

She'd also received a call from the school principal about the teaching job and graciously broke it to him that she'd accepted another position. And on Wednesday night before practice, Page informed the little Methodist church that she'd accepted the job at the symphony and would be unable to continue to work for them after Labor Day. However, she did offer to be a backup accompanist or a guest pianist beyond that, but it would depend on how much time she found herself devoting to the symphony work. Pastor Robertson appreciated the ten-week notice that Page provided and was genuinely happy for her opportunity. Vivian Backlund, on the other hand, seemed a bit agitated over the thought of losing Page. As the three sat in the pastor's study, it was clear that it would take her some time to get used to the whole idea, but she did begrudgingly congratulate Page. However, it was also clear that Vivian wasn't ready to tell the choir because she asked that Page not tell the group tonight. They all agreed to keep the news under wraps until the following week.

After the brief three-way meeting, Pastor Robertson dismissed Vivian and asked Page to stay behind.

"Page, I want to personally thank you for what you've done for our music program. But I also want to let you know that I've heard from John—a disappointed young man after receiving your recent letter. However, I must say that I don't blame you for cutting off the relationship as clearly John is far from God. I do hope you'll pray for his eventual salvation, just as I do continuously. I probably should have brought it up with you before, but I guess I was holding out some hope that your kindness might soften John's heart toward God too. That was wrong of me, for it's really God's kindness that leads to repentance."

"Oh, Pastor, I'm relieved that you are aware of all that. I didn't want to bring up the subject unless you did first. But I must confess—I need your prayers too. I have recently been on a date with another nonbeliever. Pray that I will remain strong in my faith—no compromise. And that if I am to marry someday, it will be a man who loves God," pleaded Page.

On Thursday, two sets of piano lesson parents called Page to ask her to take their young people under her wing, even if it was to be just for the months of July and August. Page had agreed to take on the two as they were teens who were taking their music seriously. The parents were willing to pay for lessons on both Mondays and Fridays every week. This would allow her to take these two young people quickly to the next level of proficiency, as long as they were getting in their practice time between lessons. Besides, every little bit was going to be needed this summer due to her small bank account.

She had also finally worked up the strength to call Jeff. Despite valiant attempts to make it through the call, she broke down after just minutes.

"Oh, Jeff, this is such a hard reality. I guess we all knew this could happen, but it was easier to be in denial that it actually would happen," Page said while wiping her nose with tissue in one hand as she sat at her kitchen table with the receiver in the other.

"Sis, this was about the only decision I could have made. They were gonna call me up; I just know it. Don't worry. I'll do my duty and come marching home before ya know it. Heck, you'll probably be pretty famous by the time I get back, so don't forget me!"

"Silly boy, I could never forget you. I'll pray for you, and I will miss you very much. I'll write to you... Let us know how to do that, won't you?"

Page was able to pull herself together enough to make plans to come home to see Jeff again before the end of the month.

Despite the tough week, Page was counting the days to Friday—the day that Gavi had indicated he'd be back from wherever he had gone. Certainly she had tried to put him out of her thoughts and keep busy, but it didn't seem to be working. Before drifting off to sleep, she would conjure up his handsome face with his warm smile, like a photograph she kept in a corner of her mind. But then the fear of his not calling would rise up like a haunting menace to whisper in her ear.

After another fitful night's sleep, Page awoke early on Friday morning. Not having to start teaching this month, she lay in bed thinking about how few of these lazy days without obligations she would have remaining. Getting up to go to the kitchen, she put some water in a saucepan to heat. Rummaging around in the cupboard, she found her small stash of tea bags and pulled one out to put into the Ohio State mug her brother had given her for a graduation gift. While the water was on, she placed two pieces of white bread into the rickety, old toaster oven her mom had passed down to her.

Sitting down at her table with tea, toast, and jam, Page was enjoying her leisurely breakfast with a good book. After finishing her meal, she headed back to continue reading on the convertible sofa bed. But having woken up so early this morning, it wasn't long before she was yawning and fell back to sleep. In a deep sleep, she came around slowly to hear the telephone ringing insistently. Rubbing her eyes, she saw her alarm clock indicating that it was now almost ten fifteen a.m. As she pulled herself out of the bed to answer, she was able to muster a "hello" in a reasonably awake tone.

"Page, it's Gavi. Did I wake you?

With eyes now wide open and her heart thumping at the sound of his voice, Page answered with an upbeat, "Yes... but I'm awake now. It's good to hear from you. But wait... how did you know my number? The last time I gave it to you to make that call to the symphony, I saw you rub it off your hand. Do you have a photographic memory or something?"

The professor audibly sighed on the other end. "Page Holden, I didn't need your phone number to make that call. I *wanted* your phone number, and it was the best excuse I could think of to get it out of you without appearing to be in pursuit."

Page giggled and replied, "Oh, I am a featherhead... I fell for it, Dr. Weiss. I'll keep your trickery in mind from now on. Imagine that—leading a girl on so!"

Now it was Gavi's turn to laugh as he responded, "Miss Holden, you are hardly a featherhead, but I'm nevertheless glad you fell for it!"

Page jumped in with, "Hey, it's Friday. You must not have gone far because you're back in town so early. Want to tell me where you went?"

Gavi was quiet for a few seconds and then picked it up there with, "Actually, I do want to tell you where I went, but how 'bout if I do that over some hamburgers and fries at Sandy's. Can I pick you up at noon?"

"Oh my, that's sounds wonderful. I'll be ready," said Page with glee in her voice.

CHAPTER 33

"A plain hamburger, fries, and a root beer float, please," was Page's answer to the gum-chewing waitress waiting to take her order. That was quickly followed by Gavi's request for the same thing. Writing down the number two on the small green ledger order slip, the waitress shuffled off toward the kitchen.

With both hands cupping her chin and her elbows on the table, Page was looking at the professor who seemed a bit subdued this afternoon. "Well, this is fun," she remarked. "I can't believe I'm eating in a restaurant again for the second time this week!"

Looking down at the table, Gavi responded, "Don't get too used to it. I'm only recently tenured and am still just an underpaid prof, remember? However, if it takes feeding you to keep your attention, I'll take up cooking if I have to. But there's more to this invitation to lunch than eating. I guess I needed to talk to someone, and I really don't have anyone to turn to."

"Go on, Gavi, I'm happy to listen for as long as you need to talk," said Page in a soft and encouraging tone.

"I came back a day earlier than I intended to because I was running away...and it was the wrong thing to do." His eyes were downcast, and he seemed unable to look at her as he continued. "I flew back to San Francisco to see my mother, Page. That's where I am originally from. Her name is Hilda. My dad was Ben, but he passed."

Page sensed that those last words were ones that Gavi was choking on, so she lowered her head and simply said, "I'm sorry for your loss. How long ago was that?"

Gavi continued, "Almost four years now, though we weren't that close. He wasn't that kind of father—more like a taskmaster. But it's my mom."

"Your mom?" asked Page. "Is she okay?"

"Apparently not. At least that's what she tells me, though I never quite know if she's playing the hypochondriac, the martyr, or not playing at all." Gavi chuckled a bit under his breath and went on. "I guess that puts her squarely in the stereotypic Jewish mother role. Hence, I don't know if she's laying a guilt trip on me for not having seen her for ten months or if she is telling me the truth."

Page was staring at Gavi in hopes he would make eye contact, which he finally did. He seemed genuinely vexed in his spirit, but she was determined to help him get all his feelings and thoughts out. "What did she tell you?" Page inquired.

"She told me that she's been diagnosed with cancer," he responded with a fear in his eyes.

"Oh dear. Are you able to talk to her physician to find out what's really going on?"

"I realized on the plane trip home that I'd have to do just that. He's been the family doc for years, but he's not an oncologist or specialist—just a GP. I don't really know who she is seeing...if it's true."

"Once again, I'm sorry to hear this. I can't say that I've ever crossed this bridge before, but whatever happens, I hope you'll let me walk with you through this situation. Gavi, I don't know your mom, but this doesn't seem like something someone would say if it weren't true."

"Yeah...I know," Gavi said as he ran his fingers through his hair, much like he did on their dinner date earlier in the week. "However, I didn't respond well to her during this visit, I'm afraid. Well, actually it's probably because I am afraid. I made up an excuse to come back home rather than stay the extra day and just try to be a good son to her."

"Now, Gavi, why would you say that? I'm sure you are a good son to her. After all, you flew back there to see her even without knowing this. That's a very kind thing to do," stated Page in her best upbeat tone.

He seemed to momentarily look past Page, so she turned to look over her shoulder only to see their food was arriving from the waitress on a big brown tray, which she set on the empty table across from their booth. As they smiled and thanked her for the delivery, the waitress shuffled off again, indicating she'd be back to check on them later.

Page had said a silent prayer when their fancy dinner arrived at the table last Saturday night, but she was really feeling compelled to pray openly right now. Not knowing how Gavi might receive that, she asked his permission to pray. He smiled wryly and said, "Of course. I could use that. Oh, and be sure to ask God to forgive me for violating Jewish dietary laws with this meal, too, would you?"

Page bowed her head and closed her eyes and began. "Lord, we thank you for this food; please bless it for our good. I also ask that you give Gavi your boundless grace and comfort during this troubling time. Help me to be a good and faithful friend to him as well. Amen."

The two ate their lunch while Page encouraged Gavi to tell her more about his upbringing. She learned he was going to be turning thirty-five this summer and that his Jewish immigrant parents had worked hard to put their late-in-life and only child through school. Though Page knew that her professor was a University of California Berkeley School of Music graduate, she learned that he had also studied Musical Arts at the San Francisco Conservatory of Music. Page was getting a clear picture of a cherished and gifted child who had spent a lifetime trying to please and live up to high parental expectations.

By the time they were down to the final slurps of their root beer floats, Gavi's spirits seemed a bit lifted. Page was even successful in getting him to laugh over stories about her contrasting family life and upbringing in the small town of Hudson. After paying the bill, he took her hand in his as they walked to his car. Putting the key in the ignition to start up the car, Gavi looked over at Page with his winsome smile and thanked her for listening... and for being a friend. All the way back to her apartment, Page just kept thinking about how many turns and twists this relationship had experienced over the course of the last nine months or so. She looked over at the handsome driver and once again could only faintly recall her tumultuous school year under his skillful tutelage. That was then, but things had changed.

CHAPTER 34

It was a hazy and humid Sunday morning that July 1 when Page turned the corner to make her way to the Methodist church. This was the day that Jeff was reporting to training, so she'd been praying for him with every step she took.

Once again, Vivian had asked her to arrive fifteen minutes earlier than usual in order to run through the anthem with the choir one last time. Page secretly wished she'd had a nickel for every time Vivian had made these requests. If nothing else, it would have kept her in laundry money.

As Page sat down on the piano bench to begin the pre-service practice session, Pastor Robertson was stopping by to pray with and for the choir members. However, this Sunday he also made the announcement of Page's new position with the symphony that would be starting in September. The members seemed a bit crestfallen at the news, but after the service, they all gathered around her to tell her how much they appreciated her and would miss her talents. Even the shy and awkward Stan Osborne stepped up, shook her hand, and then whispered in her ear, "Thank you for being so patient with us."

But the announcement of her resignation wasn't the only surprise of the day. For as Page ensconced herself in front of the organ to begin the prelude, she saw a familiar face smiling at her from the very back pew. The whole thing seemed so out of place that she did a double take to confirm that she actually saw her very own Professor Weiss.

Throughout the entire service, Page actually found herself feeling nervous about her playing. It was almost as if she was back in his small practice room waiting for him to pounce on even the slightest error in timing or expression. The one thing she took comfort in was the realization that he was likely unfamiliar with everything she played that morning. She also couldn't help but notice him slipping out of the service early—just before the benediction and postlude in fact.

Hurrying out from the back room and all the hugs and comments from choir members, Page made her way back into the sanctuary and out the front doors of the church. By now even Pastor Robertson had finished greeting and returned to his office to hang up his robe and stole. As she stood on the sidewalk outside the church, she looked everywhere for Gavi, but there was no sign of him anywhere. With eyes downcast, she went back into the small lobby of the church. She wasn't even sure why she went back in because she had all her belongings and was simply going to walk back to her apartment. Once she was standing inside, she concluded that she'd go back into the sanctuary to pray now that everyone was gone. She sat down in the exact place where she had seen the professor sitting during the service. And as she was about to bow her head, she felt a hand on her shoulder. Startled, she looked around to see Gavriel standing there.

"Gavi, I thought perhaps you'd left for good. I went looking for you...," Page started in, but her voice trailed off.

"I came back to look for you too," he responded as he came around to sit down next to her in the pew. "I suppose I was too nervous to hang around and meet people. I just wanted to see you today, and this is where I knew I could find you. Forgive me for bolting out like that."

"I understand," said Page. "Even I feel like that when I visit a church I've not been to before. It's a little intimidating to just waltz into a group that knows each other when you are the stranger in their midst. However, you're here... you did it, and I trust you don't feel too awkward sitting here with me now."

"It is a bit awkward being in a church, but I am enjoying sitting next to you. In fact, would you mind sitting even closer?" he asked while putting one arm around her.

"It felt a bit awkward for me to have you here listening to me play this morning. I kept hearing your stern voice ringing in my ear about what I should be doing differently. It took me right back to our days in your practice room on campus. You do know that you intimidated me so, don't you?" Page chided.

"Listen here, young lady," Gavi said, raising his index finger. "I was only stern to keep you on task, and to improve your art. Though I have to admit, in those last months of the academic year, being stern with you also allowed me to keep my distance. For you see, Page, I knew I was falling for you even then. What I didn't know was whether or not you'd ever be able to see me as more than just your instructor. Many times I had talked myself out of even thinking about you in that way, but then I'd see you again, and you chipped away at my resistance."

Page realized as he was talking that she was getting lost in his eyes, and his closeness to her was causing her to feel a bit warm. "Resistance?" she echoed as he placed his index finger on her lips and then moved to kiss them. It wasn't something she wanted to resist. However, she only got one kiss before Gavi sat back in the pew and pulled a piece of paper from the inside pocket of his blazer.

"I came across this flyer in the lobby; it appears to be an announcement of that summer class you were telling me about. I think I would be interested in attending, but only if you are with me every step of the way. What do you say to spending the next eight Tuesday evenings in class with this old skeptic?"

CHAPTER 35

The first Tuesday in July found Page introducing her friend Gavi to the small Bible study group in one of the small classrooms of the church. The dozen or so attendees made him feel very welcome, and Pastor Robertson invited him to question everything as they went through the scriptures. The pastor was also very pleased to have a professor from the university in attendance as the little church had seen such a marked downturn in attendance over the last few years. At the end of the first night, the pastor called for prayer requests, and that was when Gavi learned of the deep concerns Page had for her brother who was now in boot camp. As he dropped her off at her apartment that night, he just held her as she wept in his arms.

The group had decided they would start an hour earlier than the six thirty p.m. start time and have a potluck each week. But that second week, Page had been so tired she had to ask Gavi to bring something, as the best she could muster was a bag of potato chips to contribute. She didn't want him to know, but she'd been experiencing another one of her very heavy menstrual cycles, and this one just didn't seem to be coming to an end. She didn't think much of it

145

as she'd always had irregular periods and problems with cramps, back pain, and headaches since they began when she was just thirteen years old. She just couldn't remember being so tired before.

When Gavi arrived at her apartment door on the third Tuesday of July, he found a pale and even thinner-looking Page answering the door. Looking past her, he could also see the apartment was not in its usual tidy shape—even the sleeper sofa hadn't been made up. Page tried covering for it by explaining she'd been so tired this week and hardly had the strength to put the bed together, while acknowledging she'd have to clean up before her two piano students came back on Friday for their lessons. "Don't worry," she said softly. "I called my mom last night and told her to make an appointment for me to see our family doc next Saturday. I don't think it's anything urgent. I'll be fine, really."

Page picked up her Bible, notepad, and clutch to head out to the car with him when he mentioned that he'd brought a large fruit salad from home. Page sighed in the car and apologized that once again she'd not had the time or energy to make something but thanked him for remembering. Once they arrived at the church and Gavi had placed the salad in the church kitchen refrigerator, he turned to see Page sitting down on the only chair in the kitchen. As he walked toward her, she began to stand, but Gavi could see her slump to one side as she fainted away in his arms. He carried her to the sanctuary and gently laid her down on a pew, where one of the Bible study ladies could see what was happening and began fanning her face with her notepad. As Page came around, Gavi spoke firmly to her to tell her that they'd be skipping the study tonight, and he would be driving her straight to the hospital. She waved him off, but he'd hear nothing of it and picked her up to carry her to his car. She hung her arms limply around his neck, unwilling and unable to put up any argument.

Arriving at the university hospital, Gavi was barking out orders to the medics who came out to meet his parked car at the entry to the ER. Page was woozy and couldn't really make out what was happening, other than noting that she was placed on a gurney while Gavi was telling her not to worry; he'd see to everything. It was all a blur until she woke up again in a curtained-off area with smelling salts jolting her senses and attendants hovering over her taking her blood pressure and speaking quickly. They asked her some questions about her medical condition—something about diabetes, what she'd eaten, and if she had taken any medications. All she could whisper to the nurse was "bleeding for weeks now." She heard one of the attendants ask Gavi if she was his wife but never heard him respond with "That would be nice, but no, she's a friend. You'll take good care of her, won't you?"

Waking up in a hospital bed with an IV in her arm was startling, though Page was relieved to see Gavi sitting in a chair next to her bed. Before she could even get a word out, a white-coated young doctor came in the room carrying a chart. It was unclear to Page how much time had passed, but the doctor seemed to be in command now. His first order of business was to ask her if Gavi was immediate family, or did she give him permission to be in the room during discussions of her health status. Though she had planned to call her parents, right now she knew she wanted Gavi to be present and told the doctor so.

He spoke slowly when telling her that she was anemic— so much so that he was ordering a transfusion. He also told her that he suspected she might have a serious case of endometriosis, but he wouldn't know until exploratory surgery was performed to determine the severity. Page wasn't sure she knew much about that condition, but she felt like she didn't have much choice as she scrawled her signature onto consent forms that seemed to permit the surgeon to take whatever steps he deemed medically necessary.

With that, the doctor indicated that she'd be prepped for surgery soon as he would perform the work at ten a.m. She panicked—had she been here all night? No wonder Gavi appeared so ragged. The doctor turned to him and suggested that he might want to be in the waiting area around eleven a.m., though he couldn't guarantee how long he'd be waiting as it would depend on what was learned while Page was under anesthesia.

With the doctor gone, Page was suddenly self-conscious, realizing that under the white sheets and blankets, she was only wearing a loose-fitting gown that was bunched up on one side. Gavi seemed to sense her thoughts, and as he moved his chair closer to her, he pushed her bangs away from her eyes and said, "You know, you're beautiful at this time of the morning." She knew better but whispered, "Thank you for saying that. What time is it now?"

Gavi indicated that it was a few minutes after three a.m. and that he'd need to go home to shower, shave, eat, and take care of his dog that had been in the backyard all night. It was the first time he'd ever mentioned having a pet, so Page opened her eyes wide in surprise. "Yes, I have a five-year-old German Shepherd mix named Adagio—or Addy for short. You'd like her. When you get well, I'll take you to my home in Arlington to meet Addy." With that he kissed her forehead and promised to see her again when she got out of recovery.

The next thing Page could remember was hearing two female voices but seemed unable to open her eyes despite what felt like a valiant effort on her part. One of the voices called her name. "Miss Holden, your surgery is over. You're in the recovery room. It's time to wake up." Page could feel a tugging at her side but couldn't make out what it was. When she finally was able to open her eyes, she realized it was a nurse adding a warm blanket on top of her and tucking it in a bit. Page could sense that her speech was slurred as she managed to say "thank you" before having her eyes and brain go dark again.

Waking up a second time back in the room this time, her eyelashes fluttered open to see the face of the professor hovering over her while leaning on the metal bedrails that were caging her in. This time she just said, "Hmmm...a handsome angel is attending me. Perhaps I've arrived in heaven." Though her eyes closed again, she could hear him chuckle under his breath.

"First time I've ever been mistaken for an angel...and probably the last. How do you feel?"

Page tried lifting her head, but the best she could muster was turning it toward the sound of his voice. She opened her eyes again and answered, "Cold. I'm cold." In fact, she could feel herself shivering uncontrollably under the blankets. Gavi shot her a concerned look and reached for the call button that brought a nurse within about thirty seconds. He said a few words to the nurse, who then moved to Page's bedside and spoke clearly and slowly.

"Miss Holden, your body temperature is actually pretty normal at last check. You feel cold and shaky because surgery is an insult to the body. What you feel is an autonomic reaction that is quite normal after surgery. It will pass, though it may take another thirty minutes or so." The nurse reached down to check her pulse and seemed satisfied to depart once she got Page to shake her head up and down in acknowledgement of the information.

No sooner had the nurse departed than the surgeon came in the room. He was still wearing his scrubs and his mask strings were trailing down the front of his shirt. He went to pull up a stool that was at the side of the room and sat there looking at Page. She stared back at him through her chattering teeth. He appeared to look quite solemn as he took a deep breath and asked Page if she gave her permission for Gavi to be present for this debriefing on her surgery. She looked at Gavi and then back at the doctor and said, "Yes, he's my good friend, and I want him here."

The surgeon proceeded to tell Page that he'd be glad to review the information he was about to give her again when she was feeling better, but he wanted her to know now that he'd found a great deal of scar tissue and that indicated a very slim chance at her age that he could simply remove it and she'd never have another problem. In fact, he said it would be malpractice for him to have done that because she'd only end up with continued problems, pain, and even the potential of infertility and/or other complications that could arise from any pregnancy she might have.

"What I'm getting at, Miss Holden," he continued, "is that I really had no alternative but to perform a complete hysterectomy in your case. This is always a difficult message to deliver to a woman of childbearing age because, of course, it means you'll never be able to have children of your own."

Page remained calm and didn't even have any further questions for the doctor when he asked. He got off the stool and proceeded to leave the room after telling her that she'd likely be discharged within the next forty-eight to seventy-two hours, but he wanted to see her again at his medical office in one week for a follow-up. "All of that will be on your discharge papers, and I'll see you next week," he reminded her on his way out the door.

The room was quiet for several minutes as neither Gavi nor Page spoke. Her shakes and chills were starting to subside. Finally, Gavi reached over to pat her hand and asked, "You all right, kiddo?" Page turned her head toward the opposite wall so he didn't see the tear rolling out of her eye and onto the pillow.

"Sure, I'll be okay. One can hardly know what it's like to miss something you never had to begin with, I guess." But her sniffles gave her away.

He grabbed a tissue from the nightstand and handed it to her saying, "I can't possibly know what you are feeling, but I'm here for you. Remember, you're not any less of a woman than you were just a few hours ago. And, Page, you are a beautiful, intelligent, and capable woman with so much potential. Don't forget that."

CHAPTER 36

Page was discharged into the care of her parents, who took her to their home to assist in her recovery. They had taken her call from the hospital bed after her surgery and raced to be with her. The week she was in Hudson, Gavi attended the Tuesday night potluck and Bible study on his own... something he was initially nervous about. But he soon found himself comforted by the pastor and the attendees, all of whom prayed for Page, for Jeff, for him, and even for his mother's situation, which they had learned about during prayer requests in their second meeting. The Bible studies were becoming particularly meaningful to him because of the hospitality, but also because there was candid discussion of suffering, death, and the afterlife, all of which were matters weighing heavy on his mind. The news headlines in early August about Marilyn Monroe taking her own life and the swirl of recent events in his own life were causing him to seek answers—and to fervently search God's word.

By the middle of August, Page was back in Columbus and feeling much better. She was able to attend the last few classes on the book of John with Gavi. The little group had agreed to hold each other in their prayers as they departed from the last class. Each member had also written a note to Jeff for Page to send along with her first mailing to him now that she had an address.

September came in with a bang as Gavi returned to another academic year, and Page was starting her new job with the symphony. They had a wonderful extended summer with warmer days than were usual for the start of fall. Everyone was quite busy getting back into some semblance of routine, and Page had even found the time and energy to give her two students some make-up lessons to finish out her commitment to them.

And, on opening night for the symphony, Gavi had put on his best suit to travel downtown to see Page perform and then take her out to a late dinner (she'd already told him she'd be too nervous to eat beforehand). The evening was a smashing success, and after the first few minutes at the piano, Page had found herself relaxing and thoroughly enjoying herself at the keyboard.

After a cozy dinner together in which the two talked about their music, Gavi suggested that he take her to his place to meet Addy. It was late, and Page begged off, so he didn't pressure her further but told her he'd take a rain check on that visit to his place. What she didn't tell him was that though she appreciated his friendship, she was still uncomfortable with the idea of being alone with him in private quarters because of her strong attraction to him. He seemed to be reading her mind as he drove her home. Out of frustration, he challenged her on the matter.

"You're still uptight about being alone with me—after what we've been through? What's the matter Page...are you afraid we might end up having sex? What would be so wrong with that anyway?" he blurted out.

There were several seconds of silence that ensued. When she felt ready to respond, Page spoke calmly.

"I'm not afraid of sex, Gavi. I just know that it's a powerful thing, and I fully intend to reserve it for marriage, if I ever do marry. You'll have to accept that about me. But right now I just want to go home."

Despite the warm late summer evening, there was a definite chill inside the car as they drove to her apartment in silence. Gavi walked her to the door, but there were no kisses that night. In fact, it would be nearly three weeks before the two would speak again.

The great silence wouldn't be broken until mid-October. For Page, those weeks without hearing a thing from Gavriel Weiss was like the weather—growing bleaker by the day, and her mood reflected the worsening. She felt like he was making her pay the price for her strongly held beliefs. She cried, she prayed, and she even tried to forget their budding relationship. Mostly she threw herself into her work, practicing for hours upon hours during the nine a.m. to nine p.m. window that she'd promised her one wall-sharing neighbor she'd not violate for the sake of the peace. Weekly prep and productions kept her out of the apartment a lot of the time as well. The only bright spot was having received her first paycheck, which had enabled her to buy a couple of new items for her fall wardrobe, including dresses she could use for her symphony performances.

But on a moonlit night in October as she was just about to pull out her sofa bed to read a while before falling to sleep, the phone rang. Page was annoyed that someone would be calling after nine o'clock in the evening. Feeling a bit self-righteous for having been raised better than to do such a thing, she almost let it ring away without answering. However, by the fourth ring, she picked up the receiver only to hear his voice again on the other end.

"Hello?"

"Page, it's Gavi. I know it's late, but I've been working up the nerve to call you all day. I wanted to apologize for coming on so strong last month when we were together. I hope you can forgive me, because I want... I need us to be together again."

"Well, that sounds like a perfectly sincere apology. I accept it. I've missed your friendship... and your presence," said Page.

That response seemed to be all that Gavi needed to hear as he began to bring Page up to date on what had been going on in his life. Not long after their last encounter, Gavi had made the decision to transfer his mother to a Columbus nursing home where he could visit her regularly as her condition was deteriorating rapidly. He informed Page that the doctors were telling him that she may only have months to live. Page indicated that she'd been keeping his mother in her prayers and would continue to do so.

"I have told her about you," Gavi revealed.

"What have you told her?" Page inquired.

"I told her that I love you," he said as his voice dropped to almost a whisper on the phone.

Page was silent on the other end for some time before responding, "I'm guessing that didn't go over well with your Jewish mother. I know how much my own mother struggles with my seeing you. I'm crazy for you, Professor, but I should never have let my heart get this entwined with yours because of our faith differences. These are strongly held beliefs that are impossible to deny."

Gavi immediately jumped in to try to lighten things up a bit, "You're right, of course. I told you we should never have said anything to our mothers! Page, may I see you tomorrow? I'll be working but have no classes between noon and two. Among other things, I want to know if you've heard from Jeff. Could you meet me at noon for lunch at the cafeteria over at the Union?"

Page agreed to the date and after hanging up went straight to bed without reading. As she drifted off to sleep, she just kept replaying the conversation over and over in her head: "I told her that I love you..."

CHAPTER 37

Seeing each other for lunch was just another reminder of how attracted they were to each other, though Page had noted that Gavi always seemed to be a bit more buttoned-up when they were on campus. Today wasn't different in that regard. She had chalked that up to his being "on the job" and having to live up to a certain public standard when students and other faculty were around. However, even before they sat down, Gavi mentioned that the campus administration had issued a notice this morning that there might be a protest staged in or around the Ohio Union after three p.m., so he wanted to make sure they were done within an hour to keep her out of harm's way.

"What is it this time?" Page asked.

Gavi reached over to flip her bangs away from her beautiful eyes without saying a word. She was considering asking again when he finally lowered his eyes and muttered under his breath, "Seems only youth can convince themselves that they can demilitarize this hostile world."

With that, Page reached across the table for his hand, which he gladly accepted. They both felt the other was carrying such a heavy burden. She sent up a silent prayer that the Lord would give her the right words to be of comfort in some way. The two had definitely reconnected after their brief hiatus, and there was no doubt they were committed to being there for each other, particularly now that they both knew that Jeff had been sent to Vietnam.

Throughout October, Gavi was working hard and spending most evenings during the week visiting his mother. He often brought her favorite goodies and sweets, but only to entice her to eat as her appetite was waning and she'd lost quite a bit of weight. Mother and son watched the news together with great interest given the standoff that was taking place over Russian missiles in Cuba. And though Gavi was relieved to know that all United States military personnel were be removed from Laos, there was so much going on in the nation that felt like the rumblings of more unrest to come. Though Gavi was hoping his mother could be shielded from all the bad news, she seemed to be preoccupied with it as she drifted in and out of sleep on her bed.

But on the evening of November 3, Gavi called Page to ask her if she would go with him to his mother's bedside. Page felt compelled to give him all the moral support he needed, even though she was quite nervous about meeting his mother. And, as it turned out, her worst fears were confirmed. For when they entered into the dimly lit hospital room with Gavi leading the way while holding Page's hand, she could see his mother's face light up at the sight of her son, and then go dark upon seeing Page.

"Why did you bring her? Are you trying to end my life even sooner?" the woman screeched at her son.

Page couldn't take it and broke away to run out of the room with the sting of tears in her eyes. She made her way to the waiting area but quickly found herself surrounded by

Gavi's strong arms as she sobbed on his jacket. He held her for several minutes without a word and then pulled back to look her in the eyes.

"Page," he began, "I want you to stay here in the waiting area and pray. It seems your prayers are effective, and I am beginning to understand why."

"What are you saying?" Page asked while trying to pull herself together.

With his hands on her shoulders, Gavi shook her once gently—as if to help her snap out of it. He looked her directly in the eyes, and in a tone of urgency and seriousness, he said, "What I'm telling you is that this very afternoon I hit my knees and cried out to Messiah to reveal himself to me. And though I still needed you here to draw strength from, in that moment I felt assured that he was, he is, and he will answer that prayer. Do you believe me, Page? I don't know what's next for me, but I need to know that you believe me."

Page looked deep into his watery, brown eyes as he returned her gaze, while still holding onto her shoulders. Finally, she answered him, "I would never doubt you, Gavi... especially on something that life changing."

Gavi kissed her on the forehead, released her, and returned to his mother's room. Page sat down on one of the sticky vinyl benches in the area and began praying silently for Hilda, and for Gavi.

After about fifteen minutes, Gavi returned to collect Page, and they walked out to the parking lot without a word. Once they were in his car, he let out a long sigh and ran his hand back through his hair and rubbed his neck. He started the car, thanked Page for being with him through this, and then leaned over to plant a kiss on her cheek before driving her home. On the doorstep of her apartment, he held her in his arms and pleaded with her not to take his mother's comments to heart. And then he kissed her tenderly, leaving Page to wonder if any woman could ever have been so well-kissed.

CHAPTER 38

The next day was Sunday, and Gavi had agreed to park his car near her apartment building so that they could walk to church together. Many of the choir members were pleased to see Page and to meet her handsome professor. After the service, Gavi shook hands with Pastor Robertson and then proceeded to ask the pastor if he and Page might wait for him to finish his greeting duties and meet in his study for a few minutes. Page wasn't sure what prompted the request but was happy to tag along.

Within about twenty minutes, the pastor was taking off his robe and placing the garment and his stole on a wall hook in his office as he invited the couple to be seated in the guest chairs opposite his cluttered desk. It was Gavi who spoke first as he recounted the story of his encounter with God the previous day. Pastor Robertson asked Gavi several questions and then assured Gavi that his prayer was one of trust and childlike faith—the kind of soul-state that one must have to enter the kingdom of God. And like a child, Gavi asked the pastor if this meant he was a Christian. Pastor Robertson told him there was one way to be sure— one way to know for certain that his name was in the Lamb's

Book of Life. That was to pray a prayer that acknowledges sin and trusts in Christ—the spotless Passover Lamb of God who bore our sins once for all. Gavi looked over at Page, who had tears welling up in her hopeful eyes. Then he looked back at the pastor and said, "I will pray that prayer."

After the prayer, the three lifted their heads to see there were tears of joy all around. Page couldn't resist throwing her arms around Gavi and kissing his cheek. Pastor Robertson shook his hand over the desk and then rummaged around his desk drawer to pull out a brand new Bible which he presented to Gavi, who gladly accepted the gift.

Then the kind pastor mentioned to Page that Dr. John Robertson still inquired about her from time to time. He asked Page to keep praying for his son, who he said was still "hard of heart." The pastor then marveled aloud that a Jew could more readily come to Christ than a man raised in the church. "We just don't know the plans and timing of God, yet we must trust him wholly. For in the end, he only and always does what is just and right." Gavi stored up what the pastor had said in his heart, for this was a hard teaching for a new believer.

For the next six nights, Gavi attended his mother's bedside every night after work. Each time she asked him to forsake Page. He had not told his mother about his conversion, but he continued to refuse her heartbreaking requests regarding Page.

On the seventh night, he asked Page again to go with him because the doctors were now telling him his mother had just days to live. Though it was not something Page wanted to do, she mentally prepared herself for the visit and did so because she felt Gavi needed her now more than ever.

Once again as they entered the room together, Hilda turned her head toward the wall. She spoke to her son but would not look at him, asking him to promise her he'd not see Page again. Page wanted to run, but Gavi held her hand even tighter as he answered, "Mother, I cannot make that promise because I love Page."

Hilda shut her eyes tightly, and once again Page broke free to leave the room. What she wasn't present to see was a bitter Hilda opening her eyes while pleading with her son to at least promise that he'd not marry "the goy." She wasn't present to hear Gavi weep while telling his mother that there was no doubt in his mind the he would ask Page to marry him. With that, his mother closed her eyes, never to open them again or speak before her passing just twenty-eight hours later.

CHAPTER 39

Given how much Gavi had to deal with throughout the month of November, he welcomed the Thanksgiving break and eagerly said yes to Page's invitation to go home with her to Hudson to spend a few days. It was like salve to his soul to get away from campus, work pressures, and the material matters of taking care of his mother's burial and estate. Even more healing was the time he'd get to spend with Page and her parents who welcomed him as though he were family.

The Thanksgiving meal was certainly something that he'd not soon forget, and he made sure Mrs. Holden knew how much he appreciated her efforts. He and Bob Holden hit it off well, despite the differences in their backgrounds and interests. And of course, Maggie took to Gavi right away. Maggie just seemed to know a dog fancier at first sight. However, when Page and Gavi sat on the couch, Maggie insisted on sitting between the two. Page thought if she didn't know better, she'd believe that Maggie was trying to be a chaperone.

And because the Holdens had replaced the piano that Page took with her to Columbus, there were hours of incredible music emanating from the Holden residence over the holiday. Page and Gavi seemed to be in a competition to play some of the most difficult pieces possible. With those numbers that weren't committed to memory, there were plenty of classical music books around. And Gavi often insisted that Page sit close to him on the bench to be his page turner.

During halftime of the Ohio State versus Michigan game, Page and her mother had the occasion to talk in the kitchen about the relationship and Gavi's newfound faith. It was clear from some of their conversations that Mrs. Holden was attempting to gain assurance that the professor hadn't had a "convenient conversion" because he was so clearly taken with Page. But after having an opportunity to talk to Gavi alone in the kitchen, she was satisfied that he was the real deal.

After a great time (and a great football season for the Buckeyes), Page and Gavi would depart for Columbus after church on Sunday. Since Page had been raised in a Lutheran Brethren church, it was natural that Gavi had questions about why she attended a Methodist church in Columbus. Denominational and doctrinal differences were a big subject on the drive home because Gavi had so many questions as a new believer. Besides, prior to this summer, he'd only thought of Christianity in generic terms and hadn't really given it much thought beyond that.

There were other things to talk about on the way home as well because the night before they returned to Columbus, Gavi and Page had taken a walk. It was a starched cold and starry night with a waning moon. As they walked, Page worked up the nerve to ask Gavi when he realized his feelings for her.

"That's an easy one," he said. "It was definitely in the lobby of Severance Hall when I saw you talking to your doctor friend. I made a mad dash to get out of the hall because it was in that moment that I realized I didn't want to lose you to someone else. However, I also knew there wasn't much I could do until you graduated. Those thirty or so days seemed like an eternity."

"So, you were jealous? Why, Gavi, that's not something I would have ever guessed. Besides, isn't jealousy supposed to be a bad thing in a relationship?" Page asked.

"Many people say that, but I contend that's because they confuse it with covetousness. I believe that the opposite of love isn't hate, it is apathy. If I didn't care, wasn't jealous—or more likely zealous for you—then it could hardly have led to love. Remember, even one of the many names of God is Jealous, for he is jealous for his people, Israel."

Instead of responding verbally, Page stood on her tip-toes and kissed Gavi on the cheek, for her admiration and respect for the man had done nothing but grow in these last several months.

As the couple made their way around several blocks of her small hometown, they eventually came to one of the many parks in Hudson, where they sat on a bench. In the distance, they could even hear the Westminster chime of the town's clock tower. And it was upon that park bench that Gavriel Weiss asked Page Holden to marry him. Taken by surprise, Page squealed and threw her arms around Gavi, all the while saying "yes, yes, yes!" All the fuss took Gavi by surprise, though his heart thrilled to know that Page harbored no doubts about the matter.

Once he peeled her off of his neck, he confessed that he hadn't even bought her a ring yet. However, he promised to take her to Roy's back in Columbus where they could pick out rings. After kissing her, he also admitted to being concerned that she might want to think about the proposal.

"Why would you think I might need time to consider your marriage proposal?" she inquired.

"Honestly, Page, I guess I thought you might consider my having been married before, or the age difference between us, or my newness to the Christian faith to be problems."

"Honestly, Gavi, I thought you might consider my inability to bear you children, my youth, or my insistence on marriage before sex to be problems," mirrored Page with a smile.

Gavi smiled in the light of the lamp post they were sitting near and proceeded to take her in his arms and kiss her with a passion that almost frightened her. When he finally released her, she asked him what that was all about.

"I want you to know that none of that matters to me, if none of that matters to you. I just want to spend my remaining years on this earth with you—my best friend," he said looking into her eyes. Page was just about to say something when he promptly added, "Besides that, you're the sexiest thing on earth, and I can hardly keep from kissing you like that all the time." Of course, that just made her want his kisses even more. After more of those kisses, she finally got a word in edgewise.

"I love you, Professor, and I always will."

CHAPTER 40

After Gavi announced the happy news to Page's parents before they left Hudson, Mr. Holden gathered everyone together in the living room for a prayer over the couple. And Page prayed earnestly for Jeff as well as he served with over eleven thousand other troops in a very dangerous place during this holiday. The family prayer time was a bonding that later prompted Gavi to ask Page if she would teach him how to pray as he could already sense the additional dimension of intimacy it would bring to their relationship.

There were plenty of subjects to discuss over the remaining days in November, which the couple did mostly over the phone due to their busy work schedules. However, Gavi was able to make it to another one of the symphony productions to hear Page play before their season break.

Then there was the matter of a wedding date. The sticking point for the couple was over the timing, given their professional commitments. They would only have the Christmas break or sometime after graduation in June for a wedding. Page had always wanted a June wedding, but Gavi wanted to elope during the mid-December break, which was now just weeks away.

After much back and forth, they decided to do something at both points on the calendar. They agreed to have a simple, private ceremony at the Holden family home, and then they would board a plane to fly to San Francisco for their honeymoon (this would also allow Gavi to close up his mother's home and deal with other financial matters). And for Page, they would have a repeat ceremony with friends, colleagues, and family at Mirror Lake on the Ohio State campus, followed by a reception at the Faculty Club after the spring academic quarter was over in June. The compromise was sealed with Gavi promising to take Page to the newly added fiftieth state of Hawaii on their first wedding anniversary in December of the following year.

The whirlwind of putting something together within weeks, even for a small family gathering, was a bit stressful, but on the morning of Christmas Eve, before the twinkling lights on the Christmas tree in her home in Hudson, Page and Gavi repeated the vows spoken to them by the Lutheran pastor. Witnesses included her mother and father, Jean and Tom Brown, and the pastor's wife. A lovely home-cooked brunch was served up immediately after the ceremony.

The bride wore a full-skirted, tea-length, white chiffon dress, a white fur wrap around her shoulders, and silver heels. The groom wore a Madison Avenue-style, three-piece, heather-gray suit with a silver tie and black shoes. Page had followed the wedding tradition of something old, something new, something borrowed, and something blue. She borrowed Jean's pearl earrings; the garters she wore to hold up her nylon stockings were blue; the fur was something her mother had for decades; and of course, her dress was new.

Fortunately, Mr. Holden had a Kodak Brownie flash camera around to capture a few pictures of the happy couple before and after the ceremony. He'd have just enough time while they were in San Francisco to have the film developed. The highlight of the ceremony was definitely the few minutes during which the couple requested time to speak to each other before they exchanged wedding bands.

From Gavriel came, "Page, my friend, confidant, and soon to be my lifetime lover, there will be no end to my love for you. With all the good and ill that will undoubtedly come our way, I promise to make it my life's aim to please God and to please you. Thank you for saying yes to me."

With an open heart, Page responded, "Today, I am in my childhood home but will from this day forward make my home in you. Gavriel Weiss, you are God's gift to me, given only after God made you his own. I look forward to all our days together, and I take your name with gratitude and anticipation. I love you."

As Gavi kissed his precious bride upon being pronounced husband and wife, Mrs. Holden was drying her eyes, Mr. Holden was snapping another photo, and Jeff was sorely missed by all.

CHAPTER 41

The weather had cooperated well enough that Mr. and Mrs. Weiss could travel back to Columbus to the airport where they would catch a Convair 880 to San Francisco International Airport. They were wearing their winter coats over their wedding garb as they climbed the jet stairs to find their seats. Page was beyond herself with nerves as she'd never been up in a plane before. But besides feeling all the excitement of being a bride, she was feeling the thrill of what seemed like such a glamorous way to travel.

Having flown in an airplane a couple of times, Gavi made sure to give Page the window seat. His large frame hemmed her in, and she felt so secure with him next to her. As the plane eventually taxied and took off, she held onto his arm, feeling his muscular arm under his suit coat. That was her greater thrill—to know she'd soon have him to herself.

The two were served dinner by the stewardess who wore her TWA pin proudly on the white collar of her smart blue suit. Later Page snuggled on Gavi's shoulder, and the two were able to get an hour or two of sleep. Arriving many hours later, yet only nine p.m. San Francisco time, they could feel the fatigue of such a long day. Gavi carried their suitcase, and Page carried her train case as they found a cab to take them to their hotel.

As they traveled north from the airport into the heart of the city, Page was taken by all the city lights and could hardly wait to see it in the daylight. This small-town girl had only dreamed of going to San Francisco when she'd seen a travel poster in a Columbus store window a year ago. As the cab pulled into the driveway at Geary and Van Ness, Page was amazed at the sight of what was the biggest and most modern hotel she'd ever seen. Clearly, her husband had spared no expense to show his new bride the high life as they walked into the Jack Tar Hotel.

As the bellhop opened the door to their hotel room and carried their bags inside, Gavi slipped him a tip and seemed to be in a hurry to usher him right back out. He helped Page with her coat and removed his as she stood in front the big window looking at the twinkling city below. It wasn't long before she could feel Gavi standing behind her and putting his arms around the front of her.

"You know, you picked the perfect wedding dress, Mrs. Weiss. It's classy—just like you. And, it's white—as in purity— just like you," he said in a somewhat hushed voice.

Page could feel the heat of passion rising within her as she turned to face him. With her hands, she clutched the sides of his face to pull him toward her lips. For a moment, she wondered if he might think she was being too aggressive, but he seemed to enjoy her demands. Their kisses were hurried and impatient as neither one of them wanted or needed to resist any longer. While drawing her toward the bed, he was simultaneously removing his jacket and vest. She helped him remove his tie and began unbuttoning his dress shirt. With the revelation of his broad shoulders, chest, and strong arms, her heart beat faster in her own chest. Page was breathing harder as he backed her up to the edge of the bed, which she casually fell back onto as she flipped her heels off onto the floor.

"Oh, wait, my mother gave me a white silk nightgown to wear on my honeymoon night. Perhaps I should go put that on," she said in the heat of the moment.

Gavi just looked at her with his beautiful bedroom eyes and indicated that he'd be happy to see her in that nightgown—another time. Page resigned herself to being made love to even while still wearing her wedding dress, for it was clear that Gavi wasn't about to wait any longer. In fact, it all happened so fast that Page felt like she'd barely had time to breathe again before ecstasy overtook her...and then him.

CHAPTER 42

The days in San Francisco were heady. Despite the chilly December weather, it seemed so much warmer to Page than the even colder temperatures they had left behind in Columbus. But on their first Christmas Day together, they never even left the hotel room, choosing instead to order in. That night they splurged on the "Jack Tar Pound O' Prime" from the room service menu, and ice cream pie for dessert. Outside of that, each of them was the only Christmas gift the other needed.

The hotel was filled with fun amenities, including an ice skating rink on the roof. On their second full day, Page talked Gavi into skating with her, though he was hopelessly incapable of staying upright. Besides, he just couldn't take the music they played for the skaters, saying that what blared from the speakers sounded like a drunken Liberace. On the one night they had a late-night snack in the piano bar of the hotel, Page had tipped off the waiter that Gavi was a brilliant pianist. When the piano entertainer took a break, he picked up his cigarette and walked over to their table to tell Gavi he had just fifteen minutes at the keys. Gavi looked over at Page with suspicion in his eyes and told her he'd play for half that, if she played the other half. They weren't sure the clientele was all that enthusiastic about classical music, but Gavi was certain that what he and Page played was far better than anything the customers had heard that night!

The hotel was located close to the Presidio and Golden Gate Park. They ate in Chinatown, shopped, visited the wharf, and even rode the streetcar once—something Page had always wanted to do. Gavi also took Page to the theater to see *Lawrence of Arabia*, the new movie that had everyone talking. Whenever they were alone again in their hotel room, it was all Page could do to stay dressed. Gavi, who had waited so patiently for her, just couldn't seem to get enough of her now. However, none of his urgency ever frightened or bothered Page for she couldn't get enough of him either. The friends were now lovers too.

On the fourth day of their week in the city, Gavi took Page to an attorney's office where he had to sign documents and pick up new keys to the rekeyed family home on Telegraph Hill. From there, they took a cab ride that gave Page a wonderful sense of that neighborhood, though she hadn't ever heard Gavi talk about the beauty of the place. In fact, he hadn't said much about his upbringing, other than the harshness of his parents who pushed him to succeed. As the cab climbed up the boulevard, it then suddenly dashed down a small driveway behind the trees. At the end of that short, steep driveway was a beautiful gray home with large white wood-trimmed windows overlooking the foggy cityscape below.

Page almost audibly gasped as she looked at the place. "This is where you grew up?" she asked in disbelief.

"Yes, this is it," he said as he paid the cabbie, asked him to return in two hours, and got out to open her door. As she stepped out, it was beginning to drizzle, and the clouds were heavy over the horizon. When they walked up to the double-door entry, he put the key into the lock and swung open wide one of the doors while waving her in. Page walked into a massive entryway with beautiful floors covered with large Oriental rugs that she was afraid to walk on for they looked like museum pieces to her.

"Gavi, you never told me you came from a wealthy family. This is not at all what I was expecting. Are you planning on selling it? And what about these beautiful things—the artwork...," Page said as her voice trailed off into the unfinished sentence.

"I'm not sure yet, Page. Part of me wants to sell it, but the property value will undoubtedly just keep going up, so perhaps we should keep it. I suppose I didn't tell you much about my upbringing here. My grandfather and father did very well in this city. San Francisco was a good place for the Jews at the turn of the century, and still is. It's a very accepting city compared to Columbus, where during that time my parents would have been barred by covenant from buying a home like mine in Upper Arlington. But enough about that—do you like the house?"

"Like it? Why, I love it! We didn't need to stay in a hotel, Gavi. We could have just come here."

Not hearing anything but silence as she was looking at the artifacts in the well-appointed sitting room off the entrance, she turned to look at Gavi. He was looking at her with that look she was starting to understand meant, *you must be kidding*.

"Page, darling, after how my mother treated you... after what she asked of me, how would you have felt if I'd told you we were honeymooning in her home?"

"Oh yes... I guess you are right. I suppose I would have thought it odd—and perhaps even upsetting. Please don't take that wrong, Gavi. I love our hotel and all the fun we're having. It's the practical side of me who was thinking of how to save you some money on this trip."

"Since we are both practical people, I don't want you to think it didn't cross my mind. But only momentarily because I wasn't willing to ask you to do that simply for the sake of saving money," Gavi responded while moving to embrace her.

While telling her more about his childhood, Gavi showed her around the entire home, which was actually three stories, with the most beautiful view being from the rooftop garden. The place had been closed up for several months now, and there were even sheets draped over some of the beautiful furnishings, including the large Steinway grand piano in the living room. When the tour was over, he got her a glass of water in the kitchen and told her he needed to go through some things in the library desk. As he left her there, he simply indicated that she should "make herself at home," which seemed so far from anything she'd ever known.

Her curiosity drew her back to the living room where she picked at the sheet covering the piano then finally snapped it off. As it flowed gracefully to the floor, the gorgeous glossy black trim of the instrument was revealed. Page sat down on the black tufted bench and decided to play the piece she had played at her first recital during graduate school.

Within the first minute of her playing, Gavi entered the room and sat down to listen and gaze at his perfectly pos-tured wife. When she finished, he clapped. Page got up and walked over and plopped herself on his lap, but all that did was lead to making out. After a few minutes of that, he stopped kissing her and threatened to carry her upstairs to bed her again. Though Page thought about daring him, she conceded that he probably had some serious work to do, so she followed him back to the library.

Picking up a book, Page read quietly as Gavi pored over items from the large wooden desk in the room. After about twenty more minutes, he put several documents from the desk into the inside pocket of his jacket and suggested that they take a walk up the hill to see the stone tower park at the end of the road before the cabbie returned to pick them up.

CHAPTER 43

The week in San Francisco seemed to fly by, and on January 2, it was time to board a plane to return to Columbus. Upon arriving later than expected, the drive home was quiet as the two were pretty tired from their travels. However, Page was revived as she anticipated going to her new home.

Gavi had driven her through the neighborhood last month so she could see the home from the outside. He had even driven by and pointed out the home of Ohio State's football coach just several blocks from his own house. Page was excited to be setting up housekeeping, though they still had to clear out her tiny studio apartment before she could get her deposit returned from the landlord.

As Gavi turned into the driveway that went to the back of the property where there was a separate garage, he stopped the car just to the side of the house. Page looked over at him to ask him why he wasn't going to the garage.

"I would prefer to carry my wife over the threshold of the front door, if you don't mind," he said as he leaned over to give her a peck on the cheek.

As Page waited for him to come around to open her car door, she gathered her belongings. Stepping out into the

frigid darkness, she headed with Gavi toward the light of
the front porch where he took out his keys to open the door.
Then, sweeping her off her feet, he kissed her and carried
her into the foyer before setting her down and flipping on
the light. She looked at Gavi who was smiling to beat the
band, and then she saw the entry that presented a staircase
up to the second floor, as well as a hallway that led to the
back of the house. To her left was a beautiful living room
which contained a large brick fireplace, and to her right was
what appeared to be a study which contained bookshelves,
a large desk, and a gorgeous burled-wood baby grand piano.

Once again, Page was speechless at the richness of the
home, though not surprised at the dark and masculine
choice of furnishings. It looked so homey, comfortable, and
a bit lived in—something she rather expected of a bachelor.

"How about this house; do you like this one?" Gavi
asked.

"Of course, I do, Gavi. It looks like you—handsome and
a bit disheveled! It just needs a bit of housekeeping, but
I'll try not to disturb your haven too much with my female
touch."

"Listen, you do whatever makes sense to you, Page. I
don't see the mess. Just conjure up an absent-minded professor stereotype, and that's me. Now, you run along and
explore while I move the car into the garage and bring our
bag upstairs."

Page made it to the kitchen when Gavi let himself in the
back entry there. She was thrilled to actually have a kitchen,
rather than a kitchenette the size of his coat closet in the
foyer. She did explore the remainder of the downstairs and
then made her way to the second floor, where she investi-
gated the two guest rooms, the bathroom, the linen closet,
and then finally made her way to the master bedroom that

contained a queen-size bed. While Gavi was in the master bathroom, Page sat down on the bed and marveled at the thought of not having to sleep on a convertible sofa ever again.

Page could hear what sounded like the shower running in the bathroom when Gavi poked his head out from behind the bathroom door.

"It a big shower, so I just thought I'd let you know that you're welcome to join me in here," he said with a coy grin on his five-o'clock-shadowed face.

CHAPTER 44

The next few days involved picking up Addy from the neighbor's home a few doors down. That family had a young ten-year-old boy who loved Addy and was more than willing to dog sit while they were away on their honeymoon. Gavi usually paid the young boy fifty cents per day but must have been feeling generous because he slipped him an entire five-dollar bill and told him to keep the change. Page and Addy hit it off splendidly, except when Addy thought Page was getting too much of Gavi's attention. On those occasions, she would try to insert herself between the two of them.

They also spent a day clearing out her apartment and doing some cleaning before returning the key to the landlord. Since it was the weekend, Mr. Holden had driven up to Columbus in the afternoon with his truck to assist, so Gavi insisted on taking him out to dinner before he headed back to Hudson. It ended up being a quick dinner because snow was in the forecast and roads could get treacherous.

There really wasn't much integration of her things that Page needed to do because she had so few household items. The couple did, however, make the decision to turn one of the sparsely furnished guest rooms into a space for Page to have her own console piano, a small black-and-white TV, and the sleeper sofa. Gavi insisted that she might need a place to escape from him because he felt he might "smother her" with his affections.

It wasn't long before the weeks turned to months and the winter turned to spring. The happy couple had settled into their work routines, though Page's performances kept her out late on those nights. Those evenings reminded him of the many years he used to come home to an empty house. They made him lonely, but he was always happy when she got home. Often, they would sit in the kitchen and eat a late dinner together and talk about their work. During the day, Page missed Gavi who was on campus, though Addy...and the piano...were her constant companions.

The couple had also started their search for a church home in the area. They eventually settled on a church that had heavy emphasis on Bible teaching because Gavi was hungry for the Word and they both wanted good discipleship in scripture. They also took to the habit of praying in bed at the end of the day. Frequently, they would be wrapped up in each other's arms, which sometimes led to sleep even before the last "amen," and sometimes led to more strenuous activity.

One of the many things Page busied herself with were the plans for the big wedding reception, which would be held at the Faculty Club on campus. They had selected the date of June 15—just after Page turned twenty-five. Page had visited the facility several times now, sometimes meeting Gavi there for lunch. The old brick building was perfect, and they had an event coordinator she could work with on seating, food, table arrangements, and more.

As the symphony season ended for Page in mid-May, Gavi was once again getting ready for final exams and student recitals. Things were coming to a close for the summer, so the big party was a perfect way to end the school year. Page wore her pretty white dress, and Gavi wore his gray suit again. Their friends, family, and coworkers came to watch them take their vows again by Mirror Lake on that warm and sunny late afternoon. Then everyone walked up the Faculty Club stairs, through the wrought iron gate-like doors, and up the beautiful staircase to enjoy a wonderful dinner and chamber music played by some of Page's symphony friends.

The highlight of the evening was when the remaining guests gathered after dinner in an elegantly appointed sitting room in the club where there was a grand piano. Both Gavi and Page had been secretly working on their own composition, which they would reveal to each other for the first time that night. Gavi insisted that his beautiful bride go first, so Page sat down to play a romantic four-minute sonata that brought some to tears. She called it "My All To You." When she had finished playing, Gavi walked over to kiss the back of her neck. Then he took her hand to walk her over to where he had been sitting and took his place at the piano.

He explained to the crowd that his composition begins by reflecting his restlessness and brooding nature before he met Page, but the second half was his feeble attempt to help the hearer apprehend the contentment and joy he now felt in his life. He proceeded to play with a mastery that Page felt she'd never achieve. His talent, passion, and artistic expression were evident for all to see, and the crowd clapped for some time after the dramatic piece.

The happy couple departed late that evening after saying goodnight to the last remaining guests. And unlike their heated honeymoon night, they simply fell asleep in each other's arms this night after thanking God for the wonderful celebration of their love.

EPILOGUE

During their years together, Gavi and Page Weiss played concert halls in many parts the world. They played solo, as well as duets and compositions for four hands, and they always traveled together. And though she had to retire early due to arthritis in her hands, she often played the role of his page turner in their later years.

Despite their having no children, Page was known to rescue every animal that ever came her way. That presented no hardship for Gavi as he too loved animals. They were heavy financial supporters of their local church, as well as both the OSU School of Music and the veterinary college.

Just weeks after their wedding party in June of 1963, the Holden family received word that Jeff had been killed by sniper fire in the jungles of Vietnam just nine months into his tour of duty. The entire family was grief stricken, and Page mourned his loss every year of her life. There was no consoling Page's father over the loss of his son, and Bob Holden died of a massive heart attack just three years later. Ellen Holden took a job with the school district and lived a widow's life in the Hudson family home for two more decades before taking a fall. After her mother's hip surgery,

Page brought her to a rehabilitation center in Columbus so she could visit her regularly, but her mother never recovered. She passed away in her sleep to be with Jesus in April of 1986.

Gavi's faith grew stronger over the years. As one who knew his Old Testament well from his Hebrew School days, he seemed to have a special gift for opening up the scriptures to others in ways that enabled them to see Messiah as never before. He retired as dean of the School of Music in 1985 at the age of 67 and was honored by the university in many ways. Gavriel Daniel Weiss passed away at his desk at home from a sudden brain aneurysm in 1991.

More recently, Page Weiss passed away quietly in her bed at her assisted living facility where she often enjoyed listening to young people who came to play the piano for the residents. Sometimes she cried for missing him, but mostly she remembered her life with Gavi with great joy. She looked forward to the day he would greet her in heaven. In fact, she wrote a poem about that the year after he died.

"Until Death Do Us Part"

*My hand in yours upon that day, thus here and
now can hold no sway.
Separated by plans that were not ours, reunited
then by higher power.
I am here and there you flew, so all is done
while missing you.*

They all now rest in peace... and love perfected.

ALSO FROM
RAYANNE SINCLAIR

When Anne Ledwell graduates from Penn State University in 1977, her parents gift her a trip to the British Isles. She's looking forward to a break from her frustrating job search, but the last thing she expects is to fall into the arms of a handsome Scottish balladeer.

In 1980, Katerina Steiner goes to Europe to reconnect with her only living relatives. After a brief romantic encounter with an intriguing fellow tourist in Paris, Katerina returns home to find her former beau is hoping to recapture her attention. How will she choose?

Available for Kindle and in print wherever books are sold.

For more information about Rayanne's next book, please visit her website: http://rayannesinclair.com/

CPSIA information can be obtained at www.ICGtesting.com
Printed in the USA
BVOW08s1422081015

421358BV00001B/72/P